# A CORNERS CHURCH CHRISTMAS

A NOVELLA

LIFE AT THE CORNERS
BOOK 4

DONNA POOLE

Copyright ©2023 by Donna Poole

All rights reserved worldwide.

No part of this book may be reproduced in any form or by any electronic or mechanical means, including information storage and retrieval systems, without written permission from the author, except for the use of brief quotations in a book review.

Edited by Kimberlee Kiefer

Cover design by SelfPubbookCovers.com/RLSather

ISBN: 9798864003084

# FOREWORD

A wise man named Hamilton Wright Mabie once wrote, "Blessed is the season which engages the whole world in a conspiracy of love."

And blessed is the couple who engages in this conspiracy, not just at Christmas, but all year long. Their love will carry them through sunlit meadows, down dark ravines, and walk them all the way Home.

"Our task is to stand tall in God's love, secure in our place, sparkling in kindness, surrounded by his goodness, freely giving to all who come our way. You, me, and the Christmas tree. Picked, purchased, and pruned." –Max Lucado

# DEDICATION

To the people who shared Christmas stories used in this book, thank you; your stories were wonderful and added so much to this novella:
Bill Baker, Natalie Baker, Margy Barber, Deb Brammer, Deb Gramie Burgess, Sarah Griffeth Couture, Angelina Finrod Felagund Dickinson, Judy Ford, Sydney Frusti, Jim Karen Herd, Tom Kelly, Donna Krecklow, Jean Letherer, Bonnie McCall, Dianne Morris, Anita and Joe Pellerin, Pamela Plew, Mary Piarulli Post, Rebekah Rael, Joan Russell, Crystal Slezak, Ginny Slezak, Jeremiah Stump, Carolyn Wescott, Cindy Williams, and R. Marshall Wright.
To my wonderful family—my husband John, my children, and their spouses—Angie and Kim, John and Katie, Dan and Mindy, and Kimmee and Drew: your love and support inspire me every day.
To my fourteen amazing grandchildren, Megan, Macy, Reece, and Ruby; Kaleb, Kinzie, and Levi; Lincoln, Oliver, Griffin, Iris, Theo, Felix, and Walter: I'm the most blessed grandma ever.
To my editor extraordinaire, Kimmee Kiefer: I say it once again.

*You rewrote so much of this book you should be listed as co-author. Thanks for finding so many embarrassing and funny mistakes before this book was published.*

*Finally, to my readers: thank you for reading and sharing my books. If not for you, I wouldn't bother writing. I hope you enjoy this fourth book in the Life at the Corners series. If you're a new reader, don't worry, this book can be read as a stand-alone book. But if you've read the first three books, you'll find many of the characters you've grown to know and love. Happy reading!*

# AUTHOR'S NOTE

### Who's Who?

Do you find yourself scratching your head and wondering who's who in the Life at the Corners series? Whether you're a new reader or just need a refresher, here's a handy character list of the people you'll find in this book:

**Pastor Jack Daniels** —goes by J.D., current pastor of Corners Church

**Trish**—novelist and J.D.'s second wife

**Marion**— Trish's sister, the church pianist, and the church secretary

**George**—Marion's husband, former deacon at Second Baptist Church

**Jim and Darlene**—former pastor and pastor's wife at Corners Church, now deceased

**Davey**—Jim and Darlene's son, a trustee at Corners Church, works as a contractor, and father of Megan, Macy, Reece, and Ruby

**Beth**—Davey's wife, mother of Megan, Macy, Reece, and Ruby

**Megan**—Davey and Beth's oldest daughter, adult, attending a physician's assistant program

**Macy**—Davey and Beth's second oldest child, adult

**Reece**—Davey and Beth's teenage son, high school student

**Ruby:** Davey and Beth's youngest child, seven years old

**Miles**—a trustee and assistant treasurer at Corners Church, Beth's father, and grandpa to Megan, Macy, Reece, and Ruby

**JoAnn**—Beth's mother, grandma to Megan, Macy, Reece, and Ruby

**Pastor Tim and Edna**—former pastor and wife of Second Baptist Church, now retired and attending Corners Church

**Cyrus**—the oldest trustee at Corner's Church, a farmer, Trish and Marion's uncle

**Chrissy**—Cyrus's wife, Trish and Marion's aunt

**Deacon Ken**—eldest deacon at Corners Church, farmer

**Mary Beth**—an assistant treasurer at Corners Church and one of the oldest members

**Bud**—a trustee at Corners Church and a hog farmer

**Shirl**—Bud's wife, attends Corners Church

**Chuck**—a deacon at Corners Church and a contractor

**Valerie**—Chuck's wife, the clerk at Corners Church

**Thad and Caroline**—long time attendees of Corners Church

**Mark**—church treasurer and deacon at Corners Church, an electrician

**Lois**—married to Mark, attends Corners Church

**Doug**—a trustee at Corners Church and a sheep farmer

**Mattie**—married to Doug, attends Corners Church

**Dale and Jenna**—former members of Corners Church, live part of the year in the South

**Ted Carncross**—a mysterious visitor

**Cass**—J.D. and Trish's cat

# 1

## CANDLELIGHT

"My idea of Christmas, whether old-fashioned or modern, is very simple: loving others. Come to think of it, why do we have to wait for Christmas to do that?" –Bob Hope

Arms entwined and heads down against the snow, J.D. and Trish trudged across the yard and parking lot separating their home from the small, white church on the corner of two dirt roads.

"I don't recognize that little Kia," Trish said. "Do you know whose it is?"

J.D. shrugged and pulled Trish closer. "Happy anniversary week, babe. I can't believe we've been married a whole year. Do you wish we were celebrating somewhere else, like, oh, I don't know, maybe on a cruise to the Bahamas?"

Trish shook her head and laughed, and J.D.'s heart warmed.

"There's no place on earth I'd rather be than right here," Trish said.

"Even in this snowstorm?"

"Even in this. Stop for just a second. I know we're a little late, but someone is ringing the church bell, and I want to listen. You know how much I love hearing it. And I want to look at the lights in the church windows."

When they started walking again, J.D. noticed Trish's limp was getting more pronounced. The doctors had said that might happen. Her kidnapping and abuse would never really be behind them. Trish's limp was just one reminder of that. He looked down at her as she looked up a foot to meet his eyes.

"I know what you're thinking, J.D." She hugged him. "Let's just be happy tonight and think about our hundreds of blessings, not about our troubles. I'm so excited! The Christmas Eve candlelight service is my favorite of the whole year!"

"I know how much you love it; that's why I didn't cancel when this freak storm came out of nowhere. But this wind coming out of the east is making me nervous."

Trish smiled. "Hey! Look at you. You're learning, city boy. Who warned you about the east wind?"

"Cyrus."

"Cyrus? What happened to 'Uncle' Cyrus?"

"The 'Uncle' part changes based on his mood. He told me last month, after I quoted a lengthy section from D. Martyn Lloyd-Jones, to stop calling him 'Uncle.' You know what he thinks of that author. Ever since I preached from his book on Romans for a year, Cyrus gets upset if I even mention his name!"

Trish smiled. "Uncle Cyrus will get over it. He's probably forgotten about it already. And even if he remembers, he won't stay mad at you long. Aunt Chrissy won't let him."

Laughing, the two of them stomped snow off their boots and hung their coats on the rack in the back of the small country church where J.D. was the pastor.

"Ya'd think the two of ya could git here on time, livin' right next door to the church!"

The voice sounded grumpy, but there was a huge grin on the old man's face as he enveloped Trish in a hug.

"Uncle Cyrus! I didn't think I'd see you tonight!" she said.

"Whadda ya mean?" he demanded. "Ain't me and Chrissy always here every time the church doors are open?"

"The roads are getting bad, Cyrus," J.D. said. "We didn't expect any of the older people to make it out tonight."

"Who you callin' old, boy? And that's Uncle Cyrus to you!"

Trish winked at J.D. and mouthed "I told you so" before taking his hand and heading into the auditorium. As expected, there were only a handful of people there, including one visitor, an elderly man sitting alone in the back pew. Trish noticed the deep scars on the right side of his face. As J.D. started headed to the front to begin the service, she walked over to the visitor and smiled.

"Hi! I'm Trish Daniels. I'm the pastor's wife. I'm so happy to have you here with us tonight, but I'm surprised we have a visitor in this horrible weather!"

"Ted Carncross, and I, well, I um, I got a little lost in the storm," he said. "My uh...GPS on my phone wasn't working, and I saw lights on in the church, and figured I'd come in for a few minutes to get warm and try to find my way."

"Oh! Do you need directions somewhere? I'm sure one of us can—"

"No, it can wait. I'm not in any hurry."

*Why would someone want stay for a service during a snow storm instead of trying to get to wherever he's going?*

The inquisitive part of her that made her such a good author couldn't resist trying to politely get a little more information.

"So you said your name is Ted? Ted Carncross, right? You

know, we have a Carncross Road not far from here. It's named after a family who lived in this area years ago—are you by any chance related to them?"

There was an awkward silence.

When he didn't reply, Trish said, "Well, I hope you enjoy the service. It's a little different than our typical ones. Tonight is our candlelight service, and everyone who wants to participate either sings, or does a reading, or plays an instrument. But with this weather, I don't think it will be a very long service."

He nodded then looked away from her. Trish's smile faded.

*I don't think he wants to talk to me. Well, at least I tried. I hope I didn't make him feel uncomfortable. This pastor's wife thing is tough sometimes. I feel like I still have so much to learn.*

Trish walked away from the man and looked around, trying to decide where to sit. She had many choices because a lot of the pews were empty. She felt a little disappointed and worried. Most of the people were older members of the congregation; a lot of the younger families were missing.

*This service might be even shorter than I thought; there are so few people here. I know the weather's bad, but still, this service, and, well, all our other ones, seem to be getting smaller.*

Trish sat next to Pastor Tim and Edna who were still bundled in their winter coats, despite the auditorium's warmth.

"Oh no, are you two cold?" she asked.

"Ever since we passed the big eight-o mark, it seems to take us longer and longer to warm up," Pastor Tim said.

Trish glanced around the auditorium. "Where are your great-nieces and nephews?"

Edna looked sad. "Their parents got back from their mission trip last week, and the kids are out of town with them. I know they belong with their parents, but after having them with us for almost a year, our house feels empty."

Trish sighed. "The church is going to feel empty without

them too. I guess now we'll be back to only Ruby and the few other kids who come on and off."

"Oh, don't you worry about that," Tim said. "I think they're planning on attending here."

Edna squinted and looked around the auditorium. "Trish," she asked, "where'd you put your candle?"

Trish groaned. "At home! I left it on the table by the door, so I'd see it on the way out, but I forgot it! With my luck, Cass has probably knocked it on the floor by now. That will be a fun mess to clean up when I get home tonight." She looked around the auditorium as well. "Where's your candle Edna?"

Edna chuckled. "Well, I may have forgotten mine too, and apparently we weren't the only ones who didn't remember." She pointed at the table up front where space had been cleared around the nativity set for the candles. Not a single one was in sight.

Trish looked up at the piano where her sister, Marion, was playing a soft prelude of carols. No candles were on the piano either.

"How are we supposed to have a candlelight service with no candles?" Trish asked. "Should I run back home and get some?"

"Not in this snow and wind," Edna said. "Besides, we don't need candles tonight. We have the battery ones in the windows, and if there's one thing we know how to do at Corners Church, it's improvise. You know that better than I do!"

Trish sighed. "It feels like all we've been doing lately is improvising to try to keep everything going. I'm really worried about what's happening here, Edna, about our church. It seems our attendance gets smaller every year."

Edna said, "I think that attendance thing is something pastors and pastors' wives of country churches struggle to leave with the Lord. I know we did, before Tim retired, when we were at Second Baptist, and I remember Pastor Jim and Darlene did when they were here at Corners Church. Darlene wrote something about it once, and I've kept it in my Bible for many years and read it often when I started to worry. I have it with me. It's not at all Christmasy, but I think I might read it anyway during the service. Maybe it will encourage all of us."

Trish put her arm around the older woman. "I know you and Tim only started coming here last year after Pastor Tim retired, but it already feels like you've been here forever."

Tim's booming laugh filled the auditorium. "Is that a compliment? Because we could take it either way."

"Hush, Tim," Edna scolded. "J.D. is ready to start. And did I ever tell you your laugh sounds just like Santa's only ten times louder?"

Tim laughed even harder, and the sound drowned out J.D.'s opening remarks.

J.D. waited patiently with a grin for Tim to compose himself then started the service again.

"The Christmas Eve candlelight service is a long-standing tradition here at Corners Church. It predates my time by many years. Anyone may share whatever's on their hearts in any way they choose. This evening is our Christmas gift to Christ and to each other. It's a way for us to get to say to one another, 'You matter to me, and I'm glad you're a part of my life.' I guess you could say it's like a Christmas hug from one old friend to another."

"You got that right, boy! And I'll be goin' first tonight." Cyrus hollered, as he struggled to his feet. He grabbed his cane, and stomped his way to the front.

## 2

## THE SERVICE IN THE STORM

"Just as we delight in our children's laughter, so must Father in ours." –Dan MacDonald

"Smells funny in here, don't it?" Cyrus said, scowling. He whipped out a red bandana and wiped his eyes.

"Dunno why we had to get all fancied up like and not use my perfectly good cedar tree on the platform. Simple is best. I hope we don't plan to make no habit of bein' all fancy. My cedar trees is free for the cuttin', and this is the second year in a row we've spent good money on those Scotch tape pines, and I do believe I'm allergic to them!"

He wiped his eyes again.

*Uncle Cyrus,* Trish thought, *the only thing you're allergic to is change.*

Trish thought it smelled wonderful in the auditorium, even without the coffee scented candle she'd intended to bring. The wonderful scent of pine mingled with the slight aroma of garlicy pasta sauce Trish detected on Edna. Her mouth watered for just a moment as she thought about the many plates of delicious spaghetti she and J.D. had devoured at Tim and Edna's.

Cyrus loudly banged his cane on the floor, recapturing her attention.

"Next year we ain't havin' none of these bought trees. We don't need no highfalutin' Scotch tape pines when I got fields full of cedar trees free for the cuttin'!"

Someone chuckled.

"What's so funny?" Cyrus demanded, glaring.

The guilty party chose to remain anonymous. Cyrus could be intimidating, and not everyone knew what Trish did—her Uncle Cyrus might have the hide of a rhino, but he had the tender heart of a child.

Cyrus stood there, waiting for an answer that didn't come, until his wife, Chrissy, said, "It's a scotch pine, dear."

"Huh? That's what I just said. We don't need no fancy Scotch tape pines. Simple is best. That's what I told Ruby when I saw her wipin' away tears cause there weren't 'nuff kids here for the children's choir to sing. So, me and Ruby's gonna do somethin' simple instead. Come on up here, Ruby."

The little girl went and stood next to the old man. They made a startling contrast—her sparkling brown eyes and his faded blue ones, her beautiful green velvet dress with its white collar next to his work-stained overalls with one strap hanging over his shoulder, her smooth skin and his creased and wrinkled by decades spent on tractors under summer suns.

Marion started playing the opening chords, but Cyrus protested: "Hold your horses there, Marion. I'm gittin' round to it. Just give a man a minute."

Trish could see beads of sweat glistening on Cyrus's forehead. *Is...is he going to...sing?*

Surely, that couldn't be what was happening, right? It had

only been in the last two years Cyrus had been able to bring himself to pray in public, and Trish had never heard him sing, not once when she'd been growing up, not even with the congregation.

Cyrus cleared his throat. "The thing is, I dunno if I can sing no more. Used to be a real good singer, back when I was a youngin' in school, but somethin' happened and I haven't done none since. But when a friend needs you, you step up. And me and Ruby's friends. She needs someone to sing with her, so I'm gonna try."

He cleared his throat again.

Ruby slipped her hand in his and said, "Don't worry, Uncle Cyrus. I got you."

He stood a little taller. "Well, what's ya waitin' for, Marion? Don't got all night! Let's git this show on the road!"

Trish's mouth fell open when she heard Ruby's sweet voice sing the melody of "Silent Night," and Cyrus's equally sweet tenor voice carry the harmony.

The duet finished and the two of them smiled at the congregation. All was silent for a moment; then Chrissy stood and started to clap. The rest of the congregation joined her as Ruby went back to sit with her parents, Davey and Beth, and Cyrus stomped his way back with his cane to sit with Chrissy.

He paused and listened before he sat down. "Hear the east wind rattlin' those windows? That storms gittin' worse. Can't never trust no storm when the wind comes from the east."

J.D. looked concerned. "Do you all think we should maybe start heading home? We all know how the winds can whip an inch of snow into a drift a foot high on these roads. I don't want anyone to get stranded here or get into an accident on the drive home."

Voices of protest came quickly:

"I have a violin solo."

"I have a reading."

"I wanted to play my flute."

"And I want Trish to read the chapter from her new book she promised us."

J.D. smiled at Trish. He couldn't wait to hear it either. She'd been gone to a lot of meetings lately, with her editor he assumed. The book must be about finished by now.

"We can't go home yet, J.D," Trish said. "We haven't heard *A Cup of Christmas Tea.*"

Caroline Nowling, a sweet, retired teacher, read that book every year, and it wasn't Christmas for Trish until she got to hear her read it. It was getting difficult for Caroline and Thad to get out to church. He used a walker now, and she used a cane. Trish couldn't believe they'd come this stormy Christmas Eve, and she didn't want to leave until she heard Caroline read the story.

"Okay," J.D. said, putting his hands up. "I don't want to be the one to make the decision, so let's vote. Anyone who wants to go home now, raise your hand."

Pastor Tim was the only one who raised his hand. Edna stared at him, horrified.

"Tim!" she said loudly. "What in the world!"

He laughed. "What! I'm hungry." He looked up at J.D. and grinned. "I'm just kidding, son. I'm not really voting to go home, but I will say that Edna has some of her legendary meatballs waiting for me in the fridge, and I can't promise I won't be thinking about them during the rest of the service!"

Edna put her head in her hands. "Tim!"

Tim's contagious laugher filled the auditorium once more.

"Okay, darling, I'll be good," Tim said. "I promise." He kissed her cheek.

"Oh, Tim!" Edna's face grew redder, but she smiled and patted his hand.

"Now I want Edna's spaghetti too," Macy said. "I wish she'd make us some. She hasn't made us any for a really long time."

As the laughter that followed subsided, another gust of wind rattled the windows once more.

J.D. glanced toward them with concern. "You all are sure you want to risk it?"

A chorus of yeses filled the room.

"All right, I guess we're staying then," J.D. said. "Trish, do you want to read for us next?"

He winced as he watched her limp her way to the front.

*That limp is definitely getting worse.*

Trish said, "I know I'd promised I'd read you all a chapter from my new book, but it's not quite ready yet."

There were a few groans, but Trish just laughed.

"I know, I know, but sometimes the words just don't come. I've had a lot of things on my mind lately that have been distracting me."

*And that double vision hasn't made writing easy either, but I'm sure not mentioning that right now.*

J.D. stared at her, thinking. *What things are distracting you? You haven't said anything about it to me. This isn't like you, Trish.*

"What's goin' on, darlin'?" Cyrus said, leaning forward in his pew, his face full of concern. "Somethin' the matter with you?"

"I need to talk to J.D. first, Uncle Cyrus, and then I'll be talking to all the rest of you as soon as Christmas is over, but tonight I want to just celebrate together."

J.D. hoped his face didn't show the panic he felt.

*How am I supposed to enjoy Christmas after what you just said? I'm going to worry every moment until you tell me what's wrong.*

Cyrus started to protest, but Chrissy took his hand and shook her head.

"We need to let her talk to J.D. about whatever this is Cyrus, and then she'll share with the rest of us when she's ready," she said softly.

Cyrus huffed and leaned back.

Trish looked out at the concerned faces and wavered for a moment.

*Maybe I should just tell them....* But then she looked into J.D.'s worried eyes and knew she couldn't share what she needed to until she talked to him first. It wouldn't be fair.

She smiled, and said, "I want to recite something for you tonight, but I'd like Macy's help. Will you come up here, Macy?"

Macy slowly walked to the front, looking a little hesitant, but then she gave Trish one of her famous hugs.

"Macy has an unusual talent some of you may not know about," Trish said. "Ever since she was two or three, she's been able to memorize every word of every hymn. I don't know how she does it."

Macy said, "I don't know how either. I just do it."

"Do you remember when you were little, and you memorized 'In the Bleak Midwinter'? I came home from Chicago one winter that was pretty bleak for me, and you quoted it in the Christmas program and said it was your favorite song. It meant a lot to me that winter and still does. So, I wondered if you'd like to help me quote it now?"

Macy started without her, and Trish hurried to join her in saying the words to the Christina Rossetti hymn:

> "In the bleak mid-winter
> >  Frosty wind made moan,
> >  Earth stood hard as iron,
> >  Water like a stone;

Snow had fallen, snow on snow,
Snow on snow,
In the bleak mid-winter
Long ago.
Angels and archangels
May have gathered there,
Cherubim and seraphim
Thronged the air,
But only his mother
In her maiden bliss
Worshiped the Beloved
With a kiss."

Macy said, "I would have given Jesus a kiss *and* a hug too."

A few people chuckled.

"That's just what I wanted to share tonight, Macy. We can worship in lots of ways. You can worship the Lord with your hugs. I try to worship him not just with my writing but with my whole life. Before I was kidnapped, I never thought much about how short and precious life is. But now, I want to make every minute a gift to Christ, my happy minutes, and my sad minutes."

Macy hugged her. "I don't want you to be sad ever, Trish,"

"Everyone is sad sometimes, but your hugs make me feel a little better."

Macy smiled, took Trish's hand, and walked her back to her seat.

Reece stood and went to the front.

Beth leaned over and whispered to Davey, "Did you know he was going to do a special?"

Davey shook his head. "No, and I don't have the slightest idea what he's going to do."

Reece asked, "Hey, Trish, if Macy's hugs can be a gift, can laughter be something I can give?"

"Sure, Reece. Laughter is a wonderful gift."

"In that case, I have a few Christmas jokes."

Megan, home for a few days from her physician's assistant program, groaned. Reece grinned at her.

"You'll like these, Megan. What did the wise men say after they gave gold and frankincense? 'Wait, there's *myrrh*.'"

After some chuckles and a few loud groans, Reece continued. "What's the difference between the Christmas alphabet and the regular one? The Christmas alphabet has *Noel*."

This time there were more groans than laughter.

"It gets better," Reece promised. "I have some knock knock jokes. Knock knock."

The congregation played along: "Who's there?"

"Noah."

"Noah who?"

"*Noah* any good Christmas jokes?"

The laughter was genuine after that one.

"I have ten more," Reece said.

"Maybe you can save a few for later," Davey called out. "That wind is really picking up, and I think there are several more specials to go."

Reece sat down to loud applause.

"I think people liked that," he whispered to Megan. "I bet no one ever told jokes at the candlelight service before."

"They probably clapped so loudly because you were sitting down!" she whispered back.

Ruby stood back up. "Macy, come on." She tugged her older sister's hand and turned to look at everyone. "We have candy canes and tootsie rolls to give to everyone. Reece helped us buy them because he has tons of money from working construction with Dad and from helping Mark with hay last summer. Megan didn't help us buy any candy because she said PA school ate all her money. I'm never going to go to PA school. I don't want all my money eaten up."

Amidst chuckles and smiles the girls worked their way in and out of the pews handing out their candy.

After the girls sat back down, Edna went to the front. Her steps were a little slower than usual, and Trish noticed the curve in her back.

*Oh, Edna, stay with us a long, long time. We need you.*

Edna's eyes were bright under her white curls.

She said, "Darlene wrote this long ago when she was the pastor's wife here and a bit worried about declining attendance and the future of Corners Church. It isn't a Christmas reading, but I thought I'd share it tonight, just in case any of us were having the same worries she had."

She smiled, unfolded a worn sheet of paper, and began to read:

"'The Little Church that Could by Darlene Peters'

"It had been a glorious autumn day at the little church, the last day of October. The trees in the countryside were still wearing their best colors. As the sun began to lower in the west, the little church on the corner of two dirt roads sagged on its foundation and began to quietly weep. Tears streamed out of its windows and traced paths through the dust on its white sides.

"A man with a black coat flapping below his knees walked rapidly down the road. His walking stick barely touched the ground as little puffs of dirt stirred up around him but didn't seem to settle on him. His white hair touched his shoulders and made a startling contrast to the coat. He stopped suddenly, looked at the tears of the little church, and glanced up. Then he nodded, turned the corner, and sat on the church's cement steps.

'Do you mind if I rest here awhile, my friend?'

'All are welcome here,' Little Church said, fighting back sobs.

'I noticed your tears. What seems to be the problem?'

Little Church solved problems for others, it didn't share its difficulties. It studied the man sitting on its steps. He had kind, blue eyes above a neat, white beard. Little Church was sure he'd never met him before. Did he dare share his burdens with this stranger?

'Are you from around here?'

'No, my friend, I'm just passing through. I hold many secrets in my heart. Yours are safe with me.'

Out spilled Little Church's whole bitter story of better days, of days when little children filled pews, when there was barely enough room to hold all the people.

'Those were my better days. But there were so many things I couldn't do that other, bigger churches could. I couldn't have the variety of Sunday school classes. I couldn't have wonderful programs and activities for every age group; I didn't have the space or enough help. I couldn't do everything the people wanted, so they left for bigger and better. I've failed the Master, and I'm worried about tomorrow. We have so few children now; who will keep me going so I can be a light here on the corner until Jesus comes?'

'Why do you say the former days were better than these? Can you judge like our Master can judge? And as for tomorrow, like my friend Elisabeth Elliot once said, 'Tomorrow belongs to God. Tomorrow is none of your business!"

'Do you know Elisabeth Elliot?'

'Oh yes. We talk often.'

"'But... Elisabeth Elliot is dead!'

"'And you are a white frame building, but we are talking, so there is that. But remember, tomorrow is none of your business!'

"The words were stern, but the merry laughter and the kind tone soothed the heart of the little church. Where had this wise man come from?

"'You don't know which of your days will count most for eternity,' the man continued. 'God isn't finished with you yet. So, perhaps focus on what you can do in the future instead of what you can't.'

"All was quiet for a moment. A soft breeze blew from the west where the sun was a glowing, red orb. The air around the little church seemed to hint of heaven.

"The man spoke again. 'When Jesus lived on earth, he walked dirt roads. He didn't have any big programs to entertain people. He had no involved children's clubs that required many workers; he just took the children on his lap and blessed them. Jesus was a servant who taught with love. Can you listen each Sunday for the 'whisper of his sandaled feet' and follow him? Can you teach, love, and serve?'

"I can listen for him! 'Teach. Love. And Serve': That's always been my song, but fear stole my words. Thank you for singing them back to me.'

"'You're welcome,' the man said. 'I best be on my way before darkness falls.'

"He stood, stretched, and picked up his walking stick. Then he headed west down the dusty road into the sunset.

"'Wait!' Little Church called. 'I want to always remember the man who put the song back into my heart. What's your name?'

"In a voice that echoed like thunder, the man said, 'You may call me Gabriel.'

"The black coat turned brighter than the sun, and in a flash of lightning, he disappeared.

"Little Church stood tall once more on its foundation and never again forgot what it could do. For some, it would not be enough, but Little Church would teach, love, and serve with joy. And it would remember that tomorrow was none of its business."

Without another word, Edna carefully folded the paper and tucked it into her Bible. It was quiet as she returned to her seat.

After a moment, J.D. said, "I don't know how you knew we needed that, Edna. And Davey, your mom must have had a lot of love for this church, and a lot of faith too."

Davey's voice was husky. "She did. We miss her all the time, but especially at Christmas. She had a huge quote file she passed on to Megan, and Megan gave me this quote from it just the other day. I brought it to share tonight."

Davey pulled a three-by-five card from his pocket. "Ella Wheeler Wilcox wrote this 'When Christmas bells are swinging above the fields of snow, we hear sweet voices ringing from lands of long ago, and etched on vacant places are half-forgotten faces of friends we used to cherish and loves we used to know.'"

He put the card back in his pocket. "My Uncle Bruce used to tell us something I like to remember not just at Christmas but all year: 'Make memories, because someday memories are all you'll have.' And that's what we do every time we gather in this church. We make memories."

"I really like that quote, Davey," J.D. said. "And we're making another wonderful memory here tonight. Does anyone else have something to share?

Caroline walked to the front carrying a book, *A Cup of Christmas Tea.*

Trish thought, *How long has Caroline been reading this book at our Christmas Eve service? However long it's been, it's not long enough.*

Trish's eyes filled with tears as she listened to Caroline, not just reading the story, but putting her heart into it and making it come alive.

As Caroline went back to her pew, J.D. said, "Thank you, everyone, for making this a service to remember. We gave our best to the Lord and to one another too. Davey once told me his grandma loved this church and often prayed, 'God bless this little church on this little corner and make it a lighthouse until Jesus comes again.' We should all pray that. God can use little things.

"He used a little stable. Like C.S. Lewis said, 'Once in our world, a stable had something in it that was bigger than our whole world.'

"The stable held Jesus, the creator of the universe. Tonight, we've celebrated his first coming, when he came to give until he had nothing left to give. He was born in a manger so he could become a man and give his life on the cross for our sins.

"God gave us the best he had to give, his Son, and I hope you've all accepted his gift. Will you stand and recite a sweet old verse with me? You all know it, I think. It's found in the Bible, the book of John, chapter three, verse sixteen."

Young and old, voices joined in unison: "For God so loved the world that he gave his only begotten son that whosoever believeth in him should not perish but have everlasting life."

"Now," J.D. said, "as you know, we traditionally end this service by turning out all the lights and singing 'Silent Night' by candlelight. Since we have no candles, except the battery ones in the windows. . ." he paused and a few people laughed, "we won't turn out the lights. And since we all know my voice is terrible, Ruby and Cyrus, how about if you get us started?"

"We don't gotta come back up front, do we?" Cyrus asked, alarm accenting every word.

J.D. smiled. "No, right where you are is fine."

"Where are ya, Ruby?"

She came up and stood next to him. "I'm right here, Uncle Cyrus. I've got you."

Ruby started, Cyrus added his tenor, and the small congregation joined in with united love that made the angels smile.

J.D. closed the service in his traditional way, "May the depth of God uphold you. May the breadth of God enfold you. And may the love of God amaze you."

Then, as he always did when he ended a service, he raised his right hand and quoted Jude 1:24-25, "Now unto him that is able to keep you from falling, and to present you faultless before the presence of his glory with exceeding joy, to the only wise God our Savior, be glory and majesty, dominion and power...."

Trish opened her eyes. *Who is that quietly reciting the benediction with J.D.?*

To her surprise she discovered it was the visitor, Ted. She closed her eyes in time to say "Amen" with the rest of the congregation.

The echo of the amens had barely faded before Cyrus pounded the floor with his cane to get everyone's attention.

"We all best be gittin' on home before there's no way to be gittin' there. From the sounds of that wind, we're only gonna make it now Lord willin' and if the creek don't rise!"

## 3
## SHIFTING WINDS

"Plans could change in a heartbeat, though, couldn't they? The wind shifts and the clouds rush in. The air sparks and hums, and before you can even think about running, you're standing in the middle of a storm." –Anne Francis Scott

J.D. and Trish walked back to the entryway so they could say goodbye to everyone as they left. Trish winced and leaned on his arm as the familiar stabbing pain radiated from her hip down her leg. She hoped the pain didn't show on her face. It did, and J.D. looked worried.

Reece started out the door.

"I'm going to clean the snow off people's windshields so we can all hurry home like Uncle Cyrus said we should," he said.

"He's quite the kid," Trish said to J.D.

"Yes, he is!"

"That was a wonderful service, J.D.," Tim said. "Made me feel almost sad to be retired, almost but not quite. Second Baptist is doing just fine without me, and I'm happy to be here.

It was time for me to retire. Tonight sure did bring back good memories, though."

Edna chuckled. "It sure did. Remember the time you accidentally called King Herod 'Harold' in the Christmas program and then got laughing so hard you couldn't talk? Afterward I told you you'd probably preach about Harold the angel the next year!"

The entryway filled with laughter.

Edna helped Trish hand out the candy bags Corners Church filled every year, not just for the children, but for adults too. The bags held a mixture of purchased and homemade candy, and it wouldn't be a Corners Church Christmas without them.

Deacon Ken took his bag with a smile. "Any of you remember Jonas Stamp? I got a Christmas card from him the other day, and he mentioned these bags. He said while he was growing up, he looked forward to these every year, especially the homemade sweets. Jonas said, 'The ladies could really cook, and it was something they put their hearts into. People loved each other in a special way back then.'"

"I remember Jonas!" Mary Beth said. "Great kid. And people still do love each other in a special way at the Corners. Some things never change."

Edna offered Ted a bag, but he put up his hand and shook his head no.

The entryway was filled with people talking, laughing, putting on coats, hats, and gloves, and talking about their plans for Christmas the next day when Reece and a blast of snow blew back through the door.

"I'm sorry, but I had to give up," he said. "The windshields get covered with snow faster than I can brush them off. It's really bad out there; I don't think anyone's going home tonight."

"But we have to go home!" Ruby said. "Tomorrow is Christmas!"

"I don't think it can be that bad already, Reece," Davey said.

He headed out to look. It didn't take him long to return.

"Reece is right. The wind shifted northwest sometime during the service; Lickley and Tamarack Roads are both drifted shut. No chance a plow is going to come through here, not on Christmas Eve. They're going to have all they can do to keep the roads opened in town."

"I guess we're going to have to sleep on the pews," Tim said. "I don't mind, but my old bones aren't going to like it much."

"No one's sleeping here. You can all can come to our house," Trish said.

J.D. nodded agreement.

"I think I'll take my chances with the storm," Ted said. "I've already stayed here longer than I should have."

"Is that Kia out there yours?" Davey asked.

Ted nodded.

"I'm sorry, but it's buried. We could try to shovel it out for you, but there's really no point. Trish said you got lost in the storm. If you're not from this area, you probably can't guess how bad these country roads get. An inch of snow can pile up to a drift a foot deep in no time, and we've probably gotten half a foot of snow by now. No telling how deep those drifts are."

Ted sighed. *You'd probably never guess I know these roads all too well.*

"We'll try to make this one of the best Christmas Eves you've ever had!" Trish said, smiling at him.

He didn't smile back. "I think I'd really rather just stay here in the church and sleep in one of the pews if you're sure I can't travel tonight."

"But it will be cold and dark in here," Macy said. "They

turn the heat down when we aren't having church. It's nice at Pastor J.D. and Trish's. Please come."

"I'll help you walk through the snow so you won't fall," Ruby said.

He almost smiled as he looked down at the little girl who only came to his waist. As much as he disliked the thought of spending the night with strangers, he hated to disappoint this child. And his old bones didn't like the idea of a hard pew in a cold church either.

"I'll come," he said. But he didn't look happy about it.

"Good," Trish said. "Does anyone know how many of us are here tonight?"

Marion and her husband, George, did a quick head count. Davey, Beth and their four children, Pastor Tim and Edna, Cyrus and Chrissy, Deacon Ken, Chuck and Valerie, Mary Beth, Miles and JoAnn, Bud and Shirl, Thad and Caroline, Mark and Lois, Doug and Mattie, Dale and Jenna, the visitor Ted Carncross, and J.D. and Trish.

"I count thirty-one," Marion said.

"I wonder what Cass will think of that many people invading his house," Chrissy said.

"Oh, you know Cass, he loves everyone," Marion answered.

Ted scowled. *Who is this Cass person, and why didn't he come to church? Is he sick? That's the last thing I need, to catch something. I wish I could myself get out of this situation.*

"It's wonderful of you to invite us all over, Trish," JoAnn said, "but I'm sure you don't have enough blankets and pillows for all of us to spend the night."

Trish frowned. "We probably have enough pillows; J.D. is always teasing me about my collection of throw pillows, but I know we don't have enough blankets."

"What about the cots, blankets, and sleeping bags we've

been collecting for me to take to the warming center?" Doug asked. "We could use those."

"Are you sure?" Trish was hesitant. "I don't like the idea of donating things we've used."

"I'll take everything washable to the laundromat before Doug donates them when he volunteers at the center next time," Mattie offered.

Trish hugged her. "Thanks."

Doug asked, "Okay, who wants to help me pack the blankets, cots, and sleeping bags into trash bags to keep them dry and then get them over to J.D. and Trish's place?"

Ted was glad he was too old to help. He'd have all he could do to get himself next door, and he didn't want to go there. What he wanted was to be as far away from this place as possible.

*What was I thinking? Why did I think coming here tonight would help? It's only made everything worse, and now it looks like I'm going to have to spend the night with these people.*

# 4
## SNOWED IN

"Christmas is a season for kindling the fire for hospitality in the hall, the genial flame of charity in the heart." –Washington Irving

Wet boots lined up to dry inside of J.D. and Trish's house. Drenched coats hung from hangers on the shower rod in the bathroom. People crowded in front of the gas fireplace, laughing, rubbing their arms, and trying to get warm. Blankets and sleeping bags were piled in the corner of the adjoining bonus room.

"Trish, your Christmas tree is beautiful," Edna said, "and it smells wonderful!"

"It's a balsam fir," Trish answered. "I think they smell better than any other kind."

"Don't smell no better than a cedar," Cyrus grumbled, "and you coulda cut one off my property for free. Whatcha wanna go spendin' good money on somethin' you're just gonna throw away the day after Christmas anyhow?"

J.D. laughed. "The day after Christmas? I'll be lucky to get Trish to part with this tree the middle of January!"

Ted wheeled around. "That's not safe! That could cause a fire!"

Trish was surprised to see his fists were clenched, and he looked angry.

"Don't worry," she said. "I might keep the tree up that long, but I'd never light it after it dries out."

Ted sighed and looked away.

*I can't seem to say the right thing to that man,* Trish thought.

After a moment of awkward silence, J.D. said, "How about we all sit down?"

People found seats wherever they could. The second Ted sat, a big black and white cat startled him by jumping up on him. He put a hand on the cat's head, and it immediately purred and curled up in his lap.

Trish laughed. "Ted, meet Cass."

"So, what are we going to do now?" Reece asked. "It's only eight o'clock. That's kind of early to go to bed."

"I'm starving," Pastor Tim said. "You got anything to eat in this place, Trish?"

Edna rolled her eyes. "Tim, that's a bit rude, asking Trish to feed everyone. Besides, I made you supper right before we came to church."

"I'm hungry too," Ruby said, "but I didn't want to say anything and be rude, so I'm glad Pastor Tim was rude instead."

Beth sighed. "Oh Ruby!"

Trish just laughed. "We could all probably use something to eat, and I've canned enough of Edna's spaghetti sauce to feed half of Hillsdale County. But I only have one pound of pasta."

"Don't we have some boxes of spaghetti over at church that

were donated for the food drive for the warming center?" Lois asked.

Mattie nodded. "Too bad we didn't think to bring some of that with us; we could replace anything we use."

"I'll go get it!" Reece offered.

"No, Reece, you just got warm; I'll go," J.D. said.

"Best let the boy go, Preacher." Cyrus thumped the floor with his cane. "He runs track and cross country. He'll get back faster than you, Lord willin' and if the creek don't rise."

"It's not the creek I'm worried about," Davey said. "It's that wind. It's picked up even more since we got in here."

"Don't worry, Dad," Reece said to Davey. "I'll be back before you know it. There isn't a person in this room who can outrun me."

Megan loudly cleared her throat and gave her brother a pointed stare. Reece laughed.

"Well. . . . maybe you used to be able to be faster than me, Megan, but you haven't had much time to run at PA school. But if you really want to, you can go get the spaghetti?"

"No, you can go. Just be careful, and don't get lost in the storm. I'd hate to lose. . . the spaghetti."

"How many boxes should I get?" Reece asked Trish.

She looked at Edna.

"Better get whatever's there," Edna said. "Tim would eat two pounds by himself if I let him. He's done it before." She glanced at her husband. "And you don't have to look so pleased with yourself about it. It's not an accomplishment to be proud of!"

Tim laughed and everyone joined him, even Edna. It was hard not to laugh when Tim did.

Reece had his hand on the doorknob when Mattie yelled, "Better bring back Styrofoam bowls and cups, napkins, and plastic silverware too from the church kitchen. I don't imagine Trish has enough tableware and cups for all of us."

∼

A FEW MINUTES LATER, a snow-covered Reece returned with his arms full of plastic bags.

"I threw in some plates too in case we need them for anything. I could have used a sled to haul it all back," he said.

"You know, Reece, when I was a little older than Ruby, I had a big sled," Mary Beth said.

"Really?"

Reece was struggling to picture Mary Beth as a kid, but fortunately he didn't say so.

She nodded. "I must have been about ten years old. My family didn't have much money, so when a friend of Dad's showed up with a Christmas gift of a long sled for us kids, we were so excited. We didn't know a thing about how to handle it, but my siblings and I took it up the hill right away. I was in front, and I just let the thing go. We flew down the hill, jumped over a ditch, and ran smack into the side of our house. Mom and Dad came running to see if we were okay.

"After they made sure we were in one piece, my dad said, 'You know, Mary Beth, you have to steer that sled where you want it to go.'

"'Now you tell me,' I said.

"Mom and Dad laughed so hard. If I remember right, after that we went inside and ate spaghetti that day too."

∼

IT DIDN'T TAKE LONG until people were sitting on chairs and the floor, holding steaming bowls of pasta covered with red sauce and sprinkled with parmesan cheese.

"This is the best spaghetti sauce I've ever eaten," Jenna said. "How did you make this, Trish?"

"Edna taught me! It's her recipe."

"Could I have it, Edna?" Jenna asked.

"Certainly, dear!" Edna said.

"Thanks so much!"

Jenna pulled her phone out and started quickly typing while Edna shared her secret recipe: "You add olive oil to crushed tomatoes and simmer them until they start to get thick. Then add minced garlic, oregano, basil, thyme, bay leaves, Italian seasoning, a bit of sugar, and simmer it a few more hours. If it still isn't thick enough, add some tomato paste. Before you serve it, add a splash of milk and quite a bit of fresh shredded or grated parmesan cheese."

"But how do I know how much of everything to add?" Jenna asked.

"It's something you learn by doing, Jenna," Edna said. "You taste the sauce as you go along."

Edna chuckled when she saw Jenna's perplexed expression. "I'd be happy to teach you."

Several others, including Doug, asked if Edna would teach them too. While they were deciding on a time that would work for everyone, Trish leaned over to Tim.

"I know you were really looking forward to meatballs tonight," she said. "Sorry I didn't have any."

"I'll survive," he said cheerfully. "What's for dessert?"

Edna heard and groaned. "Tim, how could she possibly have dessert for all of us? You're hopeless."

He grinned. "You knew that before you married me seventy years ago."

"We haven't been married for seventy years!"

"Well, I wish we had been."

No one missed the tender smiles that passed between the old, retired pastor and wife.

"You're in luck, Tim," Trish said. "My freezer is stuffed with Christmas cookies. I was going to drop plates of them by to all of you tomorrow afternoon, but I guess since you're all here we can eat them in a little bit after they thaw. I'll start getting them out now!"

Once everyone had finished eating, Macy grabbed a garbage bag and started working her way through the crowd gathering up bowls and silverware.

"Mom," she said to Beth, "these are my new favorite dishes because you don't have to wash them. Do you think we could use them all the time?"

Beth smiled. "Probably not, Macy."

When she got to Ted, Macy collected his bowl and silverware, then lingered for a moment, studying his face. She bent close and whispered something in his ear. He brushed away a tear.

When Macy finished and sat back next to her dad, Davey asked quietly, "What did you say to the visitor?"

"I told him he doesn't have to be sad because Jesus loves him and all of us are here to help him not be sad anymore."

"Why do you think he's sad, Macy?"

"Dad! I just know. Can't you see he's sad?"

Davey gave her an astonished look then whispered something to Beth.

She nodded and whispered back to him, "I think she can sense something about Ted the rest of us can't see."

"I think maybe Cass does too." He nodded toward the cat who hadn't left Ted's lap since he'd come into the house. "And that's strange, because Cass is usually no more than two feet away from Trish."

## 5

## CAROLS BY A FIRE

"Christmas Eve was a night of song that wrapped itself about you like a shawl. But it warmed more than your body. It warmed your heart... filled it, too, with melody that would last forever." –Bess Streeter Aldrich

With dinner finished, Pastor J.D. asked, "Who'd like to sing some Christmas carols? I have an old guitar in the storage room, but I don't think anyone here knows how to play, do they?"

Macy said, "I think Mr. Ted knows how to play the guitar."

His head snapped up, and he stared at her, then smiled, a small one to be sure, but the first smile anyone had seen since he'd walked into the church. "How did you know I can play guitar, young lady?"

She shrugged. "When Pastor J.D. asked your face looked like you could play the guitar."

"Macy is very perceptive," Beth said, "but please don't feel obligated to play."

"I haven't touched a guitar in years, but I don't imagine I've forgotten how. Do you have any guitar picks, Pastor?"

J.D. nodded.

"Wait just a second here!" Cyrus said. "How's come you got a gee-tar in the storage room, J.D.? I thought I knowed everything there was about you, but I didn't know nothin' about no gee-tar playin'. You didn't play country music in a bar or somethin' before you come here, did ya, preacher?"

J.D. laughed. "No, I never played guitar anywhere. When I was still in seminary, I thought maybe I should learn to play, but it didn't take to me. I quit taking lessons, but I never got rid of the guitar."

Cyrus glared at Ted. "And hows about you? You played honkey-tonk in a bar somewhere?"

J.D. said, "Uncle Cyrus, it doesn't really matter where our visitor played the guitar, does it? If he's willing to play so we can sing Christmas carols, we should be grateful. And perhaps we should be a little more hospitable, a bit more like Jesus?"

Chrissy held her breath. If J.D. had said anything like that to Cyrus a few years ago, he would have gone through the roof, but he'd slowly been changing. She watched as her husband's scowl melted into remorse.

"Sorry, fella," he said to Ted. "I sometimes forgit my manners. We'd love to have ya play the gee-tar so as we could sing. And ever since I saw ya at church I been thinkin'. Somethin' about ya looks familiar. Have we met before?"

"Oh, I just have one of those faces that reminds people of someone they used to know," Ted said. "I'll play, but I don't think I can manage singing tonight."

"What's the matter? Ya sick or somethin'? Gotta sore throat?" Cyrus asked.

Ted shrugged, uncomfortably and didn't answer, but Macy

did: "I think his heart is sick, Uncle Cyrus. Mine gets sick too sometimes when I'm sad. It hurts."

Once again, Ted gave Macy that sad half-smile.

"You absolutely do not have to sing, Ted," J.D. said. "You playing is more than enough. Would you lead the singing, Davey?"

"I could, but it's nice having Jenna and Dale up from the south for Christmas, and you all know Dale has a great voice. Would you mind leading the singing, Dale?"

"I'd love to, Davey. I know tonight didn't go how any of us planned, but I can't think of a better way to spend Christmas Eve than being snowed in with our friends, having an old-fashioned singspiration! Who wants to choose a Christmas favorite first?"

"How about 'Silent Night' again?" J.D. asked. "I think since we're singing with a guitar, it's appropriate. Do you all know the story about how that was first sung?"

"Nope," Cyrus said with a sigh. "But gotta feelin' you're gonna tell us."

"Hush," Chrissy said. "I want to hear this."

"Okay, well go ahead, boy. Your story tellin' has improved a bit since you've married Trish. Guess some of my niece's talent's rubbin' off on ya, but keep it snappy!"

J.D. grinned. "All right, Uncle Cyrus, I'll do my best. I'm just trying to decide how to start the story."

"You've got to start with 'once upon a time,'" Ruby said. "That's how all the best stories begin, Pastor J.D."

"Okay, Ruby. Once upon a time, it is. 'Once upon a time,' on a chilly Christmas Eve just like this one way back in 1818, a pastor named Joseph Franz Mohr walked three kilometers from—"

"Kilometers? How far's three kilometers?" Cyrus asked.

"Oh, well, it's just under two miles," J.D. answered.

"Well why didn't ya just say so in the beginning?"

J.D. had planned to start his story by sharing the pastor had walked from the Austrian village of Oberndorf bei Salzburg to the town of Arnsdorf bei Laufen, but he looked at Cyrus' scowl and rethought which details to share. He started over.

"Noted, Uncle Cyrus. Let's try this again. Once upon a time, on a snowy Christmas Eve just like this one, Pastor Mohr walked almost two miles from his Austrian village to another village where his friend, Franz Xaver Gruber lived. He carried a poem with him that he'd written two years earlier. He needed a carol for the Christmas Eve mass, and he was hoping his friend Franz, a musician, could write some music for his poem."

"Hold on there!" Cyrus hollered. "You tellin' us 'Silent Night' is one of them there Catholic songs? I don't believe that for a minute!"

J.D. sighed. "Cyrus, 'Silent Night' doesn't belong only to little country churches like ours. People everywhere, from all denominations, and people who've never even attend church love that song. And if you keep interrupting me, it's going to be time for a midnight mass before I can finish this story!"

Cyrus hauled himself up out of his chair and pounded the floor with his cane.

"Chrissy, come on! You and me's leavin' this place. Just when I thought I could trust this boy, he's about to hold mass, and I'm not stayin' for it!"

Trish went to her uncle, reached up, and put her hands on his shoulders. "Uncle Cyrus, please, where would you go in this storm? Sit down, and just listen to the story. J.D. was just teasing you a little, and you know you love him under all that bluster and bellowing of yours. So please stay."

Cyrus plopped back in his seat. "Okay, darlin'. But just for you, I'll stay. That husband of yours probably don't know how to do mass anyway. He don't know a lick of French."

From the corner, a deep low chuckle turned into a real laugh. Everyone turned to see Ted laughing so hard he was wiping his eyes.

Once he'd composed himself, he said, "Oh, I'm sorry. I don't mean to be rude, but that's the first good laugh I've had in years. Mr. Cyrus, sir, I believe mass is said in Latin, and actually, most places around here you'd probably find it's fully in English now."

"Oh. Well...." Cyrus grumbled. "Don't believe he knows a lick of that Latin neither."

J.D. and Trish grinned at each other. J.D. was a fluent Latin scholar, Greek and Hebrew too, and he actually did know some French, but they didn't think it would help matters any to share that with Uncle Cyrus.

"May I continue, Uncle Cyrus?" J.D. asked. "I promise, I won't be holding mass tonight."

"All right, all right, boy. But just start where you begun, and git to the 'happily ever after' part fast now, ya here. Don't you go startin' back at the 'once upon a time part.' This here story's gittin' awful long."

"And whose fault is that?" Chrissy asked.

J.D. continued. "So, a cold Pastor Mohr had just gotten to his friend's, Franz Gruber's, house. He asked him if he could put his poem to music. In just a few hours, Franz wrote guitar accompaniment. The interesting thing about that was, Franz was actually the church organist, but he didn't write organ music that night, because a nearby river had recently flooded and ruined the organ.

"A few hours later, the two men stood in the front of the Saint Nicholas Church in Oberndorf, and the congregation there was the first to ever hear the beautiful song, 'Silent Night.' It was Christmas Eve, 1818. And now, here we are getting to sing it with a guitar on a snowy Christmas Eve—just like the Saint Nicholas Church congregation did long ago. I think that's a pretty special 'happily ever after,' don't you all?"

There were murmurs of agreement.

"We didn't get to sing by real candlelight at church, could we do that now?" Trish asked. "Oh, but do you need the lights on to see to play your guitar, Ted?"

He shook his head. "Not to play 'Silent Night' I don't. But if you're going to light candles, please be careful with them! Candles can cause fires!"

Marion helped Trish light all the candles they could find, and they kept the battery-operated candle lights in the windows on too. Then they turned off the rest of the lights, and a holy hush fell over the room as young and old voices joined together.

"Silent night, holy night!
All is calm, all is bright.
Round yon Virgin, Mother and Child.
Holy infant so tender and mild,
Sleep in heavenly peace,
Sleep in heavenly peace

Silent night, holy night!
Shepherds quake at the sight.
Glories stream from heaven afar
Heavenly hosts sing Alleluia,
Christ the Savior is born!
Christ the Savior is born

Silent night, holy night!
Son of God love's pure light.
Radiant beams from Thy holy face
With dawn of redeeming grace,
Jesus Lord, at Thy birth

Jesus Lord, at Thy birth."

Trish turned on the lights, and people smiled at each other. Then they sang another favorite song, and the harmony was beautiful, in more ways than one. Even Ted joined in.

> "'Hark! the herald angels sing,
>    'Glory to the new-born king
>    Peace on earth and mercy mild;
>    God and sinners reconciled.'
>    Joyful, all ye nations rise,
>    Join the triumph of the skies;
>    With angelic host proclaim,
>    'Christ is born in Bethlehem'
>    Hark! the herald angels sing,
>    'Glory to the new-born king.'"

"It's true what Phillips Brooks wrote," J.D. said, "'The earth has grown old with its burden of care, but at Christmas it always is young, the heart of the jewel burns lustrous and fair, and its soul full of music breaks the air, when the song of angels is sung.'"

Ted thought, *Well, that's a bunch of hogwash. My heart hasn't been young for decades.*

He played guitar for the songs that followed, but he didn't sing another word.

## 6

## COUNTDOWN TO CHRISTMAS

"Christmas is the day that holds all time together." Alexander Smith

After the notes to the last song faded, Lois said, "We should go Christmas caroling around the neighborhood sometime! Did I ever tell any of you about when my brother and I were kids and Mom heard a pastor had asked for people from area churches to show up to sing carols at Medical Care in Hillsdale the morning before Christmas?"

"You told me, and I'm tempted to include it in a book sometime," Trish said.

"Go ahead and do it, Trish! But I didn't tell anyone else?"

People shook their heads.

"Well, you all know our family has a bit of the flare for the dramatic, and Mom can sew anything. We decided to go as characters from the Charles Dickens' novel, *A Christmas Carol*. We couldn't figure out why a couple of the older ladies took one look at us, cried, and had to be removed from the activity room where we sang. In retrospect, we realized my brother looking like a realistic Ghost of Christmas Past might have been a bit much for the residents to see the first thing in the morning!"

People laughed.

After a time, conversation dwindled, and some people began looking tired.

"Should we call it a night?" J.D. asked. "We could all head to the bonus room and set up the cots and spread out the sleeping bags, and blankets, and pillows. Anyone is also welcome to sleep on the couches and recliners in there. Trish and I talked, and we want to stay in the bonus room with everyone, so our bedroom is also available. Since Edna says your snoring is legendary, Tim, maybe you two should take it?"

Tim laughed. "I'm not a bit tired. I don't know about anyone else, but I'm hungry again! Are those Christmas cookies thawed out yet, Trish? Popcorn sounds good too. You have any of that?"

"Yes to both, Tim, and I have enough hot chocolate for all of us. Whipped cream or marshmallows too if anyone wants either. I think I even have sprinkles!"

"What if someone were to want whipped cream, sprinkles, *and* marshmallows?" Tim asked.

"Tim, you're worse than the kids," Edna said, laughing.

"It's fine, Edna," Trish said with a smile. "I love filling this house with friends, and love, and laughter. It's what I told J.D. I wanted more than anything before he built the bonus room while I was...." Her face clouded over for just a moment.

She didn't have to finish her sentence. Everyone knew she was thinking of the horrible months she'd spent in the root cellar after Louise had kidnapped her.

But then her bright smile returned, and she said, "I want everyone to act just like they would at home."

"Well, in that case," Reece said, "you wouldn't happen to have any vanilla ice cream around here, would you?"

"Reece!" Megan groaned.

"What! She said to make ourselves at home!"

Trish laughed. "He's fine, Megan."

"Fine might be a bit of a stretch. You might not think so if you saw the Christmas tree he decorated and put in my room for me to find when I got home!"

"Why? Was something wrong with it?"

"Nothing was wrong with it, if you're a redneck! He made a duct tape garland, hung jumper cables off the tree, and used Grandpa's collection of old license plates for 'ornaments!'"

In the laughter that followed Reece said, "Well, you must have thought it was at least a little funny. You haven't taken it down!"

"Only because I haven't had time yet!"

"I just wanted you to know I'd missed you."

"Well maybe next time try showing me that by giving me a box of tea or a new book." But then she gave him a side hug that said, "I missed you too."

Sill smiling, Trish headed for the kitchen with Edna and Mattie following to help. Partway there she stopped, grabbed the table to steady herself, and pressed a hand over one eye.

Edna grabbed her hand. "Trish, are you all right?"

Trish nodded—grimacing in pain.

Edna whispered, "Is it that headache you told me about? Is it getting worse?"

Trish squeezed Edna's hand.

"I think maybe you need to see a doctor, honey."

Trish forced a smile. "It's gone now, Edna. I'm okay, really." But she still held the edge of the table, unwilling to explain the room-spinning dizziness that had been troubling her for a few months.

Edna and Mattie glanced at each other. They weren't convinced she was okay.

"Why don't you sit here at the table and let us get stuff around?" Mattie asked.

When she agreed, Edna and Mattie were even more worried. That wasn't like Trish.

She seemed fine though, a few minutes later.

People enjoyed the food, drank steaming cups of hot chocolate, laughed, and talked.

Under cover of the loud conversation Mary Beth said quietly to Deacon Ken, "What Cyrus said got me thinking. He's right; something about Ted Carncross is familiar. Do you know who he is?"

Ken shook his head. "A Carncross family lived in the area before my time; the road is named after them, but I don't recall hearing of any Ted. He may be one of their descendants? I don't know as I've ever met him, but I agree with you. He reminds me of someone. I just can't quite think of who."

Mary Beth chuckled. "Some people might say we're getting old, Ken. We've forgotten more than we can remember."

He smiled. "We aren't just getting old. We got old a long time ago."

As Macy gathered up popcorn and ice cream bowls, J.D. said, "If we want to keep talking, let's at least head to the bonus room, so people can be more comfortable. You're sure no one wants to go to sleep yet? Tim and Edna, how about you?"

"We aren't going to bed!" Tim said. "We don't want to miss the fun. If people aren't going to sleep right away, maybe we can tell stories about Christmas past?"

The clock on the mantle chimed twelve times.

Ruby said, "It's Christmas! Merry Christmas, everybody!"

She ran from person to person, hugging everyone. When she got to Ted, she hesitated, but only for a second.

"Merry Christmas, Mr. Ted!" she said, hugging him.

He patted her head and pressed his lips together. One tear rolled down his cheek, but in the laughter and Christmas greetings that filled the room, no one noticed. No one but Macy. And even she had no way of knowing that his one tear tied the past to the present.

# 7
## COZY IN THE BONUS ROOM

"Our hearts grow tender with childhood memories and love of kindred, and we are better throughout the year for having, in spirit, become a child again at Christmas-time." –Laura Ingalls Wilder

Because the bonus room had an entire wall of windows facing east, the howling wind made the room a bit chilly.

"Do you hear that?" Deacon Ken asked. "That snow has turned to ice. I hear it hitting those windows. I hope we don't lose power."

"I hope we don't lose any of our old trees," J.D. said. "We lost a few in the last ice storm. I'd rather have three feet of snow than an inch of ice. Ice is so devastating."

He lit the logs in the fireplace Trish had begged him to have installed. It hadn't taken much coaxing; J.D. had always wanted a real wood fireplace. The gas one was nice, but nothing beats a real wood fire on a cold winter night.

"This room is beautiful," Lois said, looking around the huge bonus room. "I love it more every time I'm here."

"When I told J.D. I wanted a room big enough so we could have everyone from church over, I never guessed we'd ever be spending the night together in here," Trish said.

"It's like a big slumber party!" Ruby said, looking around at people sprawling out on couches and cots, relaxing in recliners, and curling up on the floor in sleeping bags and in blankets.

Trish looked around at the faces she loved, trying to memorize the scene of firelight flickering, faces smiling, and her beloved J.D. looking relaxed and contented. She'd do anything to spare him another minute's worry; he'd already had more than enough to last a lifetime, but she was just going to have to trust God to get him through what was coming. And if her ordeal with Louise had taught her anything, it had taught her God is never nearer to his children than when they are hurting.

She looked around for Cass who seldom left her side, especially when a group of people was present.

*Weird, there he is, with Ted again. If any one of God's children is hurting, it's so obvious that man is. I think God brought him to us for a reason tonight.*

Trish then did what she often did, prayed God would do what she couldn't do. It was hard for her to not be able to fix something or help someone hurting, but in this case, while she hoped there was something they could all do for Ted, she believed God was the only one who could help this hurting stranger find hope and healing.

# 8

## ACADEMIC SUSPENDERS

"Christmas is a bridge. We need bridges as the river of time flows past. Today's Christmas should mean creating happy hours for tomorrow and reliving those of yesterday." –Gladys Bagg Taber

It was quiet for a while as people watched the flickering flames and listened to the sound of logs falling apart in the fireplace.

"Uncle Cyrus," Trish asked, breaking the silence, "you have a beautiful voice. Why did you quit singing?"

"Sang in choir way back when I was a kid in school," he said. "Supposed to have the solo in the Christmas concert. Never was no good with school, though. I ain't book smart, never was. Ev'rybody knows that. Two weeks before the Christmas concert, they said my grades was too bad, and they kicked me out of choir. Put me on academic suspenders."

"Suspension, dear," Chrissy said, but no one laughed. It wasn't the time.

"That was the last straw that broke the horse's back. I done quit school after that. Never went back. Big mistake. I quit singin' at the same time; I think that might have been a mistake too. But every time I tried to sing after that day, I remembered how bad I'd felt bout not gettin' to sing that solo in the Christmas concert. All my relatives was goin' to come to the program to hear me sing. So, like I said I never sung again, and I swore I'd never go back to school neither. But that was my pride talkin'. My prides done quite a bit a talkin' over the years."

He glanced at J.D. and the two men grinned at each other. Their pride and anger had kept them at odds for quite some time. But now, while they still got frustrated with one another from time to time, their friendship was solid.

"I'm glad you sang with me tonight, Uncle Cyrus," Ruby said.

He smiled. "Me too. We done a good job, Ruby."

"Cyrus, can I tell them?" Chrissy asked,

Cyrus sighed, but smiled. "You go on ahead. You're gonna whether I say so or not anyways."

Chrissy grinned proudly. "Cyrus has been working really hard for the last several years to get his GED. He didn't want to tell any of you in case he couldn't do it, but his diploma came in the mail last week!"

The room erupted in clapping, cheering, and one loud whistle from J.D.

"Okay, okay, that's enough of that," Cyrus said, waving his hand. He pounded his cane twice but his eyes twinkled. "What are we doin' focusin' on me. It's Christmas! Let's do somethin' fun."

"We could play a Christmas game we played once when I was pastor at Second Baptist," Tim said. "It's called, 'Ruin Christmas in six words or less.'

"What?" J.D. looked perplexed; he was notoriously bad at games.

"That sounds like fun!" Trish said. "I'll go first. How about this for my six words? 'I forgot to thaw the turkey.'"

"Oh, I get it now," J.D. said. "You just make up something funny using six words or less, right?"

Tim nodded. "You got it, son."

"Well, usually you make up something," Trish said, "but I really did forget to thaw the turkey, J.D. I'm sorry. Like I said earlier, I've had a lot on my mind."

*There she goes saying that again. What isn't she sharing with me?*

But J.D. knew it wasn't the right time to push her, so he squeezed her hand and said, "Turkey is overrated. I like peanut butter and salad dressing sandwiches."

Megan tried unsuccessfully not to gag. "I'm sorry, what? Is that even a thing?"

J.D. laughed. "It's what I usually ate for Christmas dinner when I was little, and lots of other dinners too. When times were good, I had potato chips to put in the sandwich. You'd think I'd hate them now, but peanut butter and salad dressing sandwiches with potato chips are still one of my comfort foods."

Ted stared at him. *What kind of family would feed their child something like that for Christmas dinner?*

But Ted didn't know the way J.D. had grown up. The rest of the people there knew about J.D.'s past, about his alcoholic father, his mother's death, and his abusive childhood. No one else was at all surprised at his childhood Christmas menu, just sad for the boy who had endured that and proud of the man he had become.

Tim cleared his throat and put a hand on J.D.'s shoulder, then said, "Anyone else want to ruin Christmas in six words or less?"

"Dad is snowbound at the airport."

"The grandkids have the stomach flu."
"I got called in to work."
"The oven just quit working."
"The dog peed on Grandma's gift."
"Tommy knocked over the tree, again."
"There are bugs in the gravy."
"The cat is licking the pie."

The room filled with laughter as more answers came, and J.D. felt relieved when he saw how often Trish was laughing. Her smile and laugh brightened the whole room.

*Maybe whatever's going on with her isn't all that bad.*

## THE MENU

"Bob said he didn't believe there ever was such a goose cooked. Its tenderness and flavor, size and cheapness were the themes of universal admiration. . . . It was a sufficient dinner for the whole family; indeed, as Mrs. Cratchit said with great delight (surveying one small atom of a bone upon the dish) they hadn't ate it all at last! Yet every one had had enough, and the youngest Cratchits in particular were steeped in sage and onion to the eyebrows." –Charles Dickens

"I know another game we could play," Pastor Tim said. "I thought of it when J.D. told us what his family had to eat for Christmas dinner. Let's plan a perfect Christmas menu where everyone can choose one thing they'd like to eat on Christmas Day. Trish, you want to keep track of the list?"

She nodded and pulled out her cell.

"Ted, you want to choose a food first?"

Ted shook his head no and looked away.

Tim looked at him sadly. *I believe that man truly hates Christmas, and I wouldn't be surprised if he has a good reason.*

Silence hung in the room for a moment.

"Hey, I have a joke about Christmas food," Reece said. "I have no *elf* control when I eat Christmas cookies."

Megan groaned.

"What! Don't like that one, Megan? How about this one? Do you love Christmas ham and Grandma's Jello? *Claus* I do."

Everyone laughed except Ted. He sat with his head lowered, and his hands between his knees.

Macy got up, went over, and sat next to him.

"It's okay not to laugh, Mr. Ted," she said. "Everyone else thinks it's a funny joke, but I don't really get it. I guess we must be friends because we both don't get it."

Ted smiled at her briefly.

"How about I start planning a menu," Edna said. "Every good meal needs spaghetti and meatballs, at least as a side dish."

"And pizza!" Reece said.

Dale laughed. "Reece, you'd really want pizza for Christmas dinner when you could have anything?"

Beth said, "Reece even eats pizza for breakfast sometimes. It's his favorite food. He'd eat it three times a day if I'd let him."

"Okay," Trish said, "so we've got spaghetti and pizza on the list. This meal is starting to sound pretty Italian."

"Well, then, we might as well add some garlic bread," George said. "Marion makes the best I've ever had."

Trish smiled at George who was sitting with his arms wrapped around her sister; Marion and George proved love has no age limit. It looks just as good on people with gray hair and wrinkles as it does on younger couples.

Trish's smiled faded. *I've never seen her so happy. I don't* want to ruin that; I don't want her to have to worry about me again.

"George, we're only supposed to pick the one thing we want the most," Marion said. "You'd pick my garlic bread over my blackberry pie?"

"I can't pick bread and pie?"

Tim shook his head no. "Just one."

George groaned. "Okay, in that case the pie wins. But if this Christmas dinner is for all of us one pie won't feed thirty-one people, not even one of Marion's."

"Megan makes the best lemon chiffon pie," Macy said. "I pick four of those."

"Tim just said you can only pick one thing, Macy," Reece said.

She frowned. "But I did. I only picked one thing. I picked Megan's pie. Four of them."

Tim smiled softly. "I'll allow it, Macy."

"Well, in that case I pick four extra-large pizzas!" Reece said.

"Then I pick four of Marion's blackberry pies," George said.

J.D. nudged Trish. "So, what's on the menu now, babe?"

"Okay, we now have Edna's spaghetti, four pizzas—"

"Extra-large!" Reece called out.

Trish laughed. "Right, four extra-large pizzas for Reece, four of Marion's blackberry pies for George, and four of Megan's famous lemon chiffon pies for Macy. What's next?"

"Well, I'm a meat and potatoes guy myself," Deacon Ken said. "How about we add a nice roast beef. Am I allowed to include the potatoes and carrots with it, Tim?"

"Is it even roast beef without the potatoes and carrots?" Tim asked.

Deacon Ken grinned broadly. "You heard the man, Trish!"

He looked around the room. "If it's for all of us, we better make it a real big one."

Trish added it, then frowned and rubbed her eyes. *Oh no, that double vision is coming more often now.*

She handed J.D. her phone. "Would you mind taking over the job of list maker?"

He shot her a worried look. "Sure, but are you okay?"

She nodded. "My eyes are getting tired. Who's next with something for the menu?"

"Let's add a whole pork loin," Bud said.

"Oh, and ham," his wife, Shirl added, "a large fresh one from one of our hogs!"

"You. . . you eat your pigs?" Macy looked like she was going to cry. "Why? We don't eat our chickens. They're our pets."

Reece said, "Well, we eat their eggs, so—"

"Reece!" Beth said, shooting him a look and shaking her head no.

"Well, Macy, two-thousand hogs are too many for us to keep as pets, honey," Shirl tried to explain.

"I guess. . ." Macy said. But she still didn't look overly convinced.

"I'll bring steak, 'nough for everybody!" Cyrus announced.

"Don't tell Macy it's from our cows," Chrissy whispered.

But Chrissy's whisper was loud, and Macy's hearing was excellent. Her eyes started to fill with tears.

"Isn't that enough meat?" Ted asked, sharply.

Everyone jumped and stared at him.

"It's just. . . you're upsetting the girl, and I don't think that's right."

Macy hugged him tightly, and though he stiffened a bit at first, after a moment he gently patted her back with one hand. She let go, and her beautiful smile came back.

"What's your favorite food, little miss?" he asked her.

"Macy already picked—" Reece started.

"Reece," Beth said once again, shaking her head.

"Maybe some mashed potatoes!" Macy said. "I love those. Mom makes the best ones. She uses like twenty pounds of potatoes. You know, I sort potatoes at the food bank, Mr. Ted."

Beth chuckled. "I usually only use five pounds of potatoes, but if I'm making potatoes for this crowd, maybe I should use twenty pounds. Maybe even thirty! What do you think of that, Macy?"

Macy laughed loudly and clapped her hands. Everyone smiled, even Ted.

"And I'll make some gravy to go with them, if that's not breaking the rules, Tim?"

"Oh, I've had your incredible gravy, Beth. It would be breaking all the rules if you didn't!" Tim said.

"Mom, maybe you could make one of your wonderful veggie platters?" Beth said to JoAnn.

"Sure! Your dad would love to help me peel the cucumbers and slice the veggies. It's one of his favorite things to do."

Miles didn't look like it was one of his favorite things to do, and a few snickers could be heard through the room.

"Well, if we're having a veggie tray, we're going to need some hot veggies to go with everything too," Lois said. "My favorite side dish for Christmas dinner is corn casserole, so I'll make one of those."

"Mine is carrot casserole," Valerie said. "So put down one of those from me, J.D."

"I'll bring potato chips," Mary Beth said.

Everyone looked at her, and Dale asked, "Mary Beth, that's your favorite thing to have at Christmas?"

"Well. . . no, not really. It's just. . . it would be the only thing I'd feel like I could bring right now, I guess. My oven's been out for three weeks now. I haven't been able to make a hot meal unless I use the microwave."

"Why didn't you say something before this?" Chuck asked. "I'll be over as soon as I can to take a look at it."

"Me too," Davey added.

"It's an electric oven, right, Mary Beth?" Mark asked.

She nodded.

"Well, then I better come along too—might be helpful to have an electrician come along with these two construction guys," he said with a grin.

Mary Beth started to protest, "But you all are so busy, and I—"

"Like I said, we'll be there as soon as we can," Chuck said. "Let us help you out, Mary Beth. You know we all love you."

Mary Beth relented with a smile, and a, "Bless you, boys."

Ted silently watched the exchange. *It's been a long time since someone has cared enough about me to do anything like that. But then again, it's been a long time since I've given a hoot about anyone else either, so what can I really expect?*

"Well if my oven is getting fixed than I want sweet potato casserole with marshmallow topping."

"Perfect!" Trish said. "Write that down, J.D. So, is our menu finished then?"

"Not yet!" Jenna said. "No one has said green bean casserole yet, and that's my favorite. So, let's add that."

"What's Cass's favorite Christmas food, Trish?" Ruby asked.

"Cheese," Trish said, laughing.

"You know what our menu is missing?" Thad asked. "Home canned pickles. I love cracking a jar of those open to go with Christmas dinner every year. Caroline and I have got all kinds back at the house. We couldn't can as much this year as we normally do with our health problems, but we have lots left from last year! Put a couple jars of those down on the list, Pastor."

J.D. read over the menu again.

"Babe, you haven't said what you want yet," Trish said to him.

"Bread," J.D. answered.

"I'd make bread for everyone too," Thad said. "I know this is all just pretend, but if we were having this meal together for real, I'd love to make bread for you all from my dad's recipes. I think most of you already know this, but he was a baker. I miss baking from his recipes; I wish I felt up to it more."

"We haven't had your bread in so long, and it's so good!" Macy said. "I'm sorry you haven't felt good." She left Ted and went and sat between Thad and Caroline so she could hug them both.

"Oh Macy," Caroline said, squeezing her tightly, "your hugs make both of us feel much better already."

Mattie smiled at the three of them and then said, "You know, I just got an idea. What if we tried to actually have this meal together sometime around Christmas next year and invited the community to join us? We could have it in the fellowship hall! We've been praying about ways to use that space as more of an outreach. I'd help cook everything, and I could set up all the tables and decorate."

The response was enthusiastic from almost everyone. J.D. looked over and saw Ted's expression. The man looked so sad.

"Maybe you could back next Christmas too?" he said to Ted. "We'd love to have you visit us anytime."

Ted looked away. *I never should have stopped here this time, and I'm sure not making that mistake again.*

## 10

# THE COOKIE PASTOR

"When we recall Christmas past, we usually find that the simplest things, not the great occasions, give off the greatest glow of happiness." –Bob Hope

A contented silence fell over the room, and the only sounds were the wood crackling in the fireplace as sparks shot upward—and a sudden loud snore from Pastor Tim. Edna chuckled and poked him.

"Dear, Trish and J.D. said we could use their bedroom. Why don't we go to bed?"

Tim jumped. "Huh? What? I'm not a bit tired! Let's share some Christmas stories!" He slapped his knee. "Who's got a good one?"

"Trish, can I have some paper and a pencil?" Ruby asked.

"Sure! What for?" Trish said. She stood to look through her desk, silently thanking God that she didn't feel dizzy and that her vision had returned to normal.

"I want to write down everybody's stories! When I grow up, I want to be a writer just like you."

Megan grinned. "Hey! You don't want to be a physician's assistant like me?"

Ruby shook her head. "No. I told everybody earlier, remember? Your school ate all your money. I don't want that! You always say you never have any money."

Megan laughed. "Well, I hope I will someday!"

Trish handed Ruby a notebook and a pencil. "I hate to tell you this, Ruby, but most writers don't have any money either. Do you know how many books I had to write before I started making any money?"

Ruby shook her head no.

"Twenty."

"Twenty!" Ruby looked horrified. "That would take forever! Maybe I'll be a pastor instead. Are you rich, Pastor J.D.?"

He laughed. "Hardly, Ruby. Well, not rich in money, but I'm rich in another way."

"How can you be rich if you don't have any money?" Ruby asked.

"In friends, love, and happiness," J.D. said. "And that's what really matters."

"I like those things!" Ruby said. "Okay, I've decided. I'm not going to be a writer anymore. I'm going to be a pastor."

"Ruby, you can be a pastor," Reece protested.

"Why!" Ruby said.

"Have you ever seen a girl pastor at our church? I don't think so."

"Well, then I'm just going to be the first. I'll be. . . a pastor to the old ladies! There are a lot of them in our church, aren't there, Pastor J.D.?"

J.D. tried not to laugh. "Um, well, Ruby, what exactly would you do if you were a pastor to the old ladies?"

"I'd go visit them and read them stories. Mom says I'm a

good reader. Oh, and I'd take them cookies. Mom could make them."

"Oh, I see how this is going," Beth said, rolling her eyes and smiling. "Well, if I make the cookies, do I get to be a pastor too, Ruby?"

Ruby nodded. "Of course! Mom, you can be my second pastor. You can drive me to visit all the old ladies! And we can visit them together and fix all their problems! Like, if the old ladies are sad, I'll tell them one of Reece's stupid jokes."

"Hey!" Reece said.

Ruby continued as if Reece hadn't said anything: "And if they're sick, you can make them some of your homemade chicken noodle soup. And I can help them fold all their laundry or do their dishes, as long as they don't have too many. And if they've stopped coming to church for a while, I'll just tell them they have to come back! If they need a ride, you can go pick them up every Sunday, Mom!"

"Sounds like being your second pastor would keep me pretty busy, Ruby," Beth said.

Cyrus pounded the floor with his cane. "Hey now!"

J.D. stiffened, waiting for the old man's protests to Ruby's desire to be a "pastor." He quickly started trying to come up with what he could say to defuse the situation; the last thing he wanted was for Ruby's feelings to get hurt, especially on Christmas.

"Sounds to me like Ruby would make a fine pastor to the old ladies!" Cyrus said. "Preacher J.D., whadda ya think?"

J.D. tried to keep the relief from showing on his face. "Well, I don't think I've ever heard of a seven-year-old pastor, but I think it sounds like Ruby would make a great one!"

"Can I do it, Mom? Dad? Can I be a pastor to the old ladies this summer when school's out? Will you drive me to visit them, Mom? No one would even have to give me any money to go. I'd just do it because I love old ladies!"

Marion chuckled. "I think any of us would love a visit from you, Ruby, even if you do call us 'the old ladies.'"

"I want to be an old lady pastor too!" Macy announced. "I like the old ladies. Maybe they'll give us cookies when we visit them, Ruby!"

"No, Macy," Ruby said with a facepalm, "we are supposed to give them the cookies!"

"Well, if they wanted to give us cookies, I think it would be nice to let them."

Cyrus pounded his cane. "If there's gonna be cookies, what about us old men? I mean us men. Don't we get no cookie pastor?"

"You could have some of the cookies we bring Aunt Chrissy," Ruby said, "if she wants to share with you, Uncle Cyrus."

"Maybe if you're good, Cyrus," Chrissy said with a twinkle in her eye.

"What do you mean, woman!" Cyrus bellowed. "I'm always good!"

"But what about Deacon Ken, Ruby? Who's going to make him cookies?" Macy looked distressed. "And Mr. Ted needs some cookies too, if he stays."

"Don't count on me being here, Macy," Ted blurted out. "I wouldn't want to stay here if it were the last place on earth!"

While some people might have been offended or hurt, Macy just looked at him a moment.

Then she said quietly, "Well, I hope you can find a last place on earth where you'd be happy, Mr. Ted. I think everybody should get to be happy."

Ted looked at her for a moment before quickly turning his face and wiping his eyes with the back of his hand. Then he stood and went to one of the windows, staring out into the darkness.

The silence that followed Ted's outburst was uncomfortable.

After a couple seconds, Tim tried to lighten the mood, and slapped his knee again. "Well, the night's not getting any younger! And I thought we were going to tell some Christmas stories. J.D., you got one for us?"

## 11

## THE TOBOGGAN

"We would get on our toboggan, a boy would give us a shove, and off we went! Plunging through drifts, leaping hollows, swooping down upon the lake, we would shoot across its gleaming surface to the opposite bank. What joy! What exhilarating madness! For one wild, glad moment we snapped the chain that binds us to earth, and joining hands with the winds we felt ourselves divine!" –Helen Keller

"Oh, I don't think anyone wants to hear my Christmas stories, Tim." J.D. protested. "You know I don't really have any happy ones."

Trish squeezed his hand. "You don't have to tell a story if you don't want to, babe. I could tell one instead?"

"Well, maybe there's one. . . let me think a second."

J.D. got up, threw another log on the fire, stretched, and looked into the flames. Then he came back and sat by Trish.

"Yeah, I think I have one I can share, but I don't know how to begin this."

"Remember what I told you, Pastor J.D.?" Ruby asked.

"You've got to start with 'once upon a time.' That's how all the good stories start. And they end with 'happily ever after.'"

J.D. chuckled and rubbed the two lines between his eyes.

"Okay, Ruby. I'll try. 'Once upon a time,' I got a Christmas present, but only once. I think I must have been about six; it was just before my mom died. Christmas Eve that year, I broke off a small cedar branch I found on a little tree at the edge of the woods and brought it inside.

"'Can we put this on the table and decorate it?' I asked Mom. 'Maybe Santa will see it and leave me a present! The other kids at school all get presents.'

"Dad laughed. He was drunk, as usual.

"'Ain't no Santa comin' round here, boy, and if he does, I'll shoot him between the eyes.'"

Ruby gasped. "Your dad was going to shoot Santa?"

J.D. grimaced. *Maybe I should have left that out; I didn't think that part through.* "My dad wasn't a very nice man, Ruby. But don't worry. He didn't shoot anyone."

"Phew," Ruby said, looking greatly relieved. "What happened then?"

"Well, then my dad left. I don't know where he went, most likely to one of the bars down the road, probably the one that had a flashing sign that said, 'Always Open.'

"Mom put that little cedar branch in a canning jar and told me it was a 'fine little tree.' Then she popped some popcorn, and we made it into a tiny garland to hang on it. I colored some white paper red and green, and Mom and I made a paper chain to put on the tree. Then Mom made a little paper angel for the top of it—we traced my hands on some paper and used it to make the wings. We sang Christmas carols together when we were done decorating, and I told her probably for the hundredth time that year what I wished I could have for Christmas more than anything. I wanted a wooden toboggan, big enough for four people.

"See, when my dad was out drinking, my mom would read to me. She's who got me to love books and reading."

J.D. paused for a moment and looked toward his and Trish's expansive collection of books lining the wall. *I wish you could see this, Mom. You'd love it. I wish you could see who I became, in spite of everything.*

Trish reached over and squeezed his hand, looking worriedly into his eyes.

J.D. smiled sadly and squeezed her hand back. *And I wish you could have met Trish, Mom. You'd have loved her.*

J.D. cleared his throat and continued: "That winter, Mom had been reading me *The Story of Helen Keller*, and I wanted a toboggan just like Hellen Keller had in the book. I thought if I could take one to the sledding hill, maybe someone might want to ride down with me, and I might finally make some friends. When I told my mom that she teared up. And I didn't understand it at the time, but I do now. She hugged me and agreed a toboggan would be a wonderful way to make friends.

"I wanted one so much I used to dream about what Helen Keller had said about how flying down a hill on a toboggan felt like 'joining hands with the wind.' I was a strange little boy."

"I think it sounds like you were a wonderful little boy," Edna said with tears in her eyes.

J.D. stood and went back to the fire, holding his hands out to it.

"Is... that the end of the story?" Ruby asked. "You forgot to say, 'and we all lived happily ever after.'"

"Well, Ruby, my story doesn't end all happy; it's sad too. But I can stop there if you want."

Ruby thought for a moment, and then said, "No, I want to hear what happens."

"Are you sure?"

Ruby nodded.

J.D. glanced over and Davey and Beth, and they nodded as well, so J.D. continued: "On Christmas morning when I woke up, I didn't know if my dad would be there or not; sometimes he was gone for days. And sometimes, most of the time, when he was there, I wished he wasn't; Mom felt the same way."

"Why?" Ruby asked. "I'd be really sad if I woke up on Christmas, and my daddy wasn't there."

J.D. searched for a moment on how to explain. "That's because you have a really good daddy, Ruby. My dad wasn't like your dad. He had a very bad temper. And sometimes he was really mean to me and my mom."

"Oh." Ruby looked down. "I'm sorry your daddy wasn't a nice daddy."

J.D. teared up for a moment. "Thank you, Ruby." He cleared his throat again. "But this Christmas, Dad was there at the kitchen table with an empty bottle next to him, and my mom was making pancakes.

"'Merry Christmas, J.D.!' she said. 'This is the day we celebrate the birth of Jesus. He— '

"Dad slammed his fist down on the table and slowly stood. 'There will be no more talk about Jesus in this house! How many times have I warned you—'

"He headed for my mom, and I ran and stood in front of her. I knew I couldn't protect her; I was too little, but at least I could let her know someone loved her.

"My dad called me a list of words that morning no six-year-old should hear, but I'd heard them since I'd been born. He strode toward me, anger twisting his face. I looked at him and put up both my little fists.

"And then he did something I'd never expected. He

laughed. My bravado had worked, that one time. It never would again.

"'Them pancakes about ready?' he asked my mom.

"Dad saw me staring at the empty spot under the canning jar tree while we ate.

"'You didn't think Santa would actually come, did you, boy? Told you if he showed up here, I'd shoot him.'

"Then he laughed like he'd told the funniest joke in the world. I knew what he might do to me if I cried, but I couldn't help it. Tears ran down my cheeks.

"'J.D., go outside, and look under the trailer,'" Mom said.

"I remember that minute like it was yesterday. It was snowing outside, and I could see my breath. I was so excited that I'd run outside without my jacket, but I didn't notice the cold because as soon as I spotted it, I felt warm all over. There, under the trailer, sat a toboggan, even bigger than the one I'd dreamed about. It was a Flexible Flyer with a red rope.

"I reached for it, but never got a chance to touch it. Before I could grab the rope, my hand was smacked away, and my father was looming over me.

"He started screaming at my mom, 'Where'd you get the money for that, woman?'

"When my dad screamed, I was terrified. It was so loud, and I knew people in the other trailers in the trailer park where we lived could hear him, but no one ever came to help us.

"I ran to my mom, afraid he'd come after her again, but he didn't. He just stood there between me and my mom and my toboggan, smirking. It was an ugly, twisted look on him.

"Mom's voice shook. 'I saved a little from grocery money every week. And I used the birthday money my folks sent me.'

"Dad said, 'You know better than to keep any money from me, but I'll forgive you this once since this is perfect timing. I used up the last of my cash at the bar last night. Had to tell my boys I couldn't celebrate with them today, but I'll bet one of them would be happy to buy this sled off me to give to one of their kids. One this fancy will probably get me enough to buy a Jack Daniels for everyone and at least three for me! Merry Christmas to me!'

"Then I stood there and watched as Dad flung my new toboggan into the back of his rusted pick-up and roared up the road toward the bar. I wasn't warm all over anymore. I was burning hot. That was the day I realized I hated him.

"Then I heard my mom crying.

"'I'm so sorry, J.D.' she kept saying.

"'It's okay, Mom. I'll get even with him someday when I get big. You just see if I don't.'

"She cried harder. I didn't understand. Didn't she want me to make him pay for everything he'd done to us?

"'Oh, J.D.," she said through her sobs, 'please, don't be like him. Don't let bitterness ruin your life. Come with me, and let's talk to Jesus about it.'

"But I didn't. I ran into my room. I slammed my door, and I cried. And I spent all day on Christmas thinking of all kinds of mean things I could do to my father. But I was just a little boy, small for my age, and when he came home in one of his mean drunk moods late that night, I couldn't protect myself or my mother from him. He didn't do much to me, but my mom wasn't so lucky. That was the last Christmas I had with my mom. She died late the next fall."

J.D. glanced around the room. Everyone but Ted knew most of his story about what his life had become once his mother had died. Things had taken a very dark turn for him once she was gone. By the time he was a teenager he had an alcohol addiction, and the bitterness toward his father his mother had so desperately wanted him to avoid had festered in him for years. Even after he'd trusted the Lord as Savior, he'd almost ruined his life and his ministry as a pastor until just a few years ago when he'd found a way to leave it with the Lord. Only after that had he finally been able to find the peace, joy, and happiness he knew his mother had always wanted for him.

The room was quiet for several moments until Ted abruptly broke the silence: "A man like your father deserves to rot in hell! He didn't deserve the family he had!"

J.D. was shocked by Ted's reaction. The man didn't even know him, but clearly his story had struck a chord with him. Ted's fists were clenched; his face was red, and tears were streaming down his cheeks.

"I hope you did get even with him!" Ted said.

"No, Ted, I never did. And I'd give anything to have a chance to tell my dad that I forgive him and that God loves him."

Ted scoffed and turned back to look outside at the storm.

He'd been just like J.D. and all these people once. He'd loved people, loved Christ, put all his faith in God, and what had that gotten him? Those days were gone forever, and the man he'd once been? Well, that man was dead; he'd been dead for thirty years.

J.D. wasn't sure what to do so he tried to change the subject. "Does anyone have a story about when Pastor Jim was here? Ted, Jim was the pastor here for fifty years before I came. That's pretty impressive, right, fifty years?"

Ted turned slightly and nodded but didn't say anything.

As the light fell across Ted's face, Cyrus, Deacon Ken, and Mary Beth found themselves staring at him again. He noticed, and they quickly glanced away. They hadn't intended to stare, but they'd all been caught up yet again trying to figure out why he looked so familiar.

Deacon Ken felt the need to try to explain, "Sorry, Ted, it's just that some of us feel like we've seen you somewhere. Have you maybe visited our church before?"

"You do look awfully familiar, Ted," Chrissy said.

Edna and Tim nodded; they'd been trying to figure out where they knew him from as well.

Ted took a step back into the shadows and crossed his arms. "People are always getting me confused with someone else."

Davey could tell the man was uncomfortable, and he didn't want the tense situation to get any more awkward.

"Pastor Jim was my dad, Ted, and I have tons of stories I could share about while he was pastor here. One of them is about Deacon Ken's dad. Would anyone like to hear that one?"

"I would!" Ruby said. "But Dad, Deacon Ken is awful old. If you knew his dad, you must be getting kind of old too!"

Davey laughed. "Thanks a lot, Ruby!"

"Hey, I'm not getting any younger myself," Mary Beth said, "so let's hear it Davey."

"Some of you have probably heard part of it before," Davey said. "It's the one about the Christmas tree."

## 12

## OH CHRISTMAS BUSH, OH CHRISTMAS BUSH

"Before we took down the tree each year, Dad would always say a prayer that we would be together the next Christmas. I cling to that prayer, which serves as a reminder that it's important to be grateful in the present for the people you love because, well, you never know." –Catherine Hicks

"Dad," Ruby asked, "does your Christmas tree story start with 'once upon a time,' and end with, 'happily ever after?'"

"Well, it depends on how you look at it. My mom, your Grandma Darlene, didn't think it ended happily ever after at first, but I think she changed her mind later."

Ruby sighed. "I wish I could have known Grandma Darlene better, but she went to heaven when I was little. I guess I was just born too late."

Beth teared up. Ruby had been born late in life for her and Davey, so she wouldn't have grandparents or parents as long as their other children would. But born too late? She pulled the little girl and the soft blanket she was holding onto her lap.

"Ruby, please don't think that; you were born at just the right time."

Ruby snuggled close for a moment and then sat up straighter and wiggled free of Beth's embrace.

"I have to write down all these stories, Mom," Ruby said as she plopped down on the floor, "because I'm going to be a writer like Trish."

"I thought you was gonna be the cookie pastor!" Cyrus said.

Ruby looked perplexed, then smiled. "I'm going to be both! I'll write stories so I have something good to read the old ladies! Tell the story about the tree, Dad."

Davey laughed. "Okay, Ruby. Every year, Deacon Ken's dad, Pete, invited Mom and Dad to cut a cedar tree in one of his fields—"

"See!" Cyrus interjected. "I'm not the only one who appreciates a good cedar!"

Trish smirked.

Davey tried not to laugh and continued: "Mom and Dad were really grateful because there was no way they could afford to buy our family a Christmas tree. Some years the cedars were more brown than green, but they always smelled good."

"See!" Cyrus said, staring pointedly at Trish.

"I never said they didn't, Uncle Cyrus!" Trish said, giggling.

"Cyrus Goodright," Chrissy said, "if you keep interrupting, the sun will be coming up before Davey gets to finish this story, and I for one would like to hear it!"

Cyrus put his hands up. "Okay, okay, darlin', don't go gettin' your suspenders twisted. I'll be good."

"How do you spell suspenders?" Ruby asked.

"Don't go writin' that down!" Cyrus said, turning red. "Though you t'was just writin' down the stories! Keep goin', Davey!"

Davey's brown eyes twinkled. "Anyway, one year Mom and Dad went to Pete's, and they cut a short, scrawny little cedar, and we kids let Dad know just how disappointed we were in the size.

"Dad shrugged and said, 'Sorry, kids. It was the best one I could find. The others were too tall to get in the house.'

"My sister, April, made up a song we sang to the tree that year."

Davey cleared his throat, grinned, and sang, "Oh Christmas bush, oh Christmas bush, how ugly are thy branches!"

People chuckled.

"The next year, Dad vowed to find a better one. Probably so he could avoid any more original musical compositions critiquing the tree. It was unusually warm that year, and Mom and Dad had to trudge through mud in Pete's field to get to the trees. Dad was determined to find one we kids would like, so he kept walking and walking. Finally, Mom got tired and told him just to pick the best one he could find and get it done so they could get the tree home and pick us up from school on time.

"'What about this one?' Dad asked. 'It looks pretty good, don't you think?'

"'It doesn't look any worse than the rest of them,' Mom said.

"Dad sawed through the trunk until the tree fell into the mud. When he picked it up, though, he only had half a tree. He hadn't realized he was cutting through two trees joined by one trunk. So, he brought home what looked to him like the best half and put the flat side up against the wall."

The room filled with laughter, but Ruby frowned.

"This doesn't sound like a 'happily ever after' story to me, Dad."

"Just wait, I'm getting to that part," her dad said.

"Okay," Ruby nodded, "I won't get my suspenders twisted like Aunt Chrissy."

George snorted, and Marion elbowed him. Chrissy raised her eyebrows at Cyrus. He turned even redder.

Davey smirked. "The next year Mom decided we were going to have a real tree. She knew where she could get her favorite kind, a scotch pine—"

"Hey!" Macy interrupted. "Scotch tape pines are Uncle Cyrus's favorite too, right Uncle Cyrus?"

The room exploded into laughter.

At this this point, Cyrus was redder than anyone had ever seen him. He cleared his throat.

"Bit partial to cedars myself, Macy."

"Oh," Macy said, confused, "you've just talked about them so much, I thought they were your favorite."

Chrissy raised her eyebrows at Cyrus again as he sunk further down into his recliner.

Davey managed to regain his composure. "Like I was saying, Mom wanted our family to have a real Christmas tree that year. And she found a spot that sold them for ten dollars a tree, but ten dollars was a lot of money back then, more than we spent on groceries for a whole week for our family. Dad had no idea where we'd get that kind of money.

"Then, one day, Mom came running in from the mailbox. Dad said she was as excited as a kid; someone had sent them ten dollars. She begged; Dad gave in, and off they went to buy the 'real' Christmas tree.

"On the way to get the tree Dad started worrying.

"'What are we going to say to Pete when he asks us to come cut our tree? I don't want to hurt his feelings.'

"Mom didn't want to hurt his feelings either. She loved Pete as much as Dad did, but she could already picture that beautiful scotch pine in the corner of our living room.

"'Don't worry, honey,' she said. 'We'll think of something to tell Pete that won't hurt his feelings.'"

Ruby gasped. "So, Grandma and Grandpa got the tree? And they didn't hurt Mr. Pete's feelings? And it was a 'happily ever after' Christmas? Right?"

Davey smiled down at his little girl. "Not exactly, Ruby. A sudden snow squall made the roads really slick. Mom and Dad had to go up a little hill to get to the Christmas tree farm, and there was a line of cars ahead of them. Mom watched, horrified, as one by one those cars slid into the ditch."

"'Be careful, hon—' she started to say, but before she could finish her sentence their car was in the ditch too."

Ruby sighed. "Dad, this story isn't as sad as Pastor J.D.'s, but it sure isn't very happy."

"Hey! Give me time! I still didn't get to the 'happily ever after' part yet!

"Dad didn't know how he was going to get out of the ditch with the little car he was driving, but then he saw a big truck coming down over the hill. He watched as the truck stopped and pulled each car from the ditch, one at a time. But then he noticed money exchanged hands each time, and that made him nervous; the only money they had was Mom's ten dollars for the Christmas tree.

"After a long time, the truck driver finally arrived at the end of the line where Dad was waiting.

"'Want me to pull you out?'

"'How much?'

"'Ten bucks.'

"In one way, Dad was relieved; he didn't know what he would have done if the guy had said fifteen dollars, but he was sad too. He looked at Mom. She sighed, opened her wallet, and gave him her money. Then, they turned around and headed home."

"Dad!" Ruby protested. "That's the end of the story? That's not happy!"

"It's not the end! The next day the phone rang. Pete asked if they'd like to come cut a cedar tree. Mom told me later that as she and Dad walked hand in hand through the fields and heard the snow crunching under their boots, she was so relieved she hadn't had to hurt Pete's feelings. Dad found a beautiful tree that year. Cyrus is right, nothing smells as good as a cedar tree."

Cyrus's face lit up, and Chrissy kissed his cheek.

"We had a wonderful Christmas with mostly handmade gifts and lots of love and laughter," Davey said. "It was one of our best ever."

Ruby's eyes sparkled. "And did you live 'happily ever after,' Dad?"

"We did live 'happily ever after,' Ruby, and I'm still doing it!" he said, grinning at Beth.

Ted was still standing, staring out into the darkness.

*Good for you. I'm still living in this hell on earth.*

Ted could see the scene behind him in the reflection in the window—the firelight, the Christmas tree lights, the laughter. He watched as couples young and old held hands and friends exchanged smiles.

*There's no love like that left on earth for me, no 'happily ever after,' as that little girl keeps saying—no one who cares if I'm here or not, if I live or die.*

Cass wound around his feet and purred. Ted looked down and something in him stirred for just a moment. He bent down and picked up the large cat. Cass laid his head on his chest and purred.

"Do you have a cat, Ted?" Trish asked.

He shook his head. "Not anymore. Did once."

Lois had been watching, and smiled at Trish and J.D. "That cat of yours really is something. Mark and I used to have a cat."

Cass's ears picked up when he heard the word "cat" and he looked at Lois like he was waiting for the rest of the story.

Lois laughed. "Look at your cat, Pastor J.D. I think he understands what I'm saying."

"He understands way too many words," J.D. said, "and 'f-o-o-d' is one of them. I can't believe he hasn't jumped into someone's plate or bowl by now. He must be trying to impress Ted."

Lois smiled. "Tiger, our big orange tabby, was a sweet boy. He never did anything bad except one Christmas."

"Oh no, what happened?" Trish asked.

"Well, it was the first Christmas Mark and I were married, and we'd bought some beautiful decorations for our first Christmas tree. We were getting ready to decorate it together when my Grandma Pat stopped by to give us an early Christmas gift. She wanted us to have some of the ornaments she and my grandpa had put on their first tree."

"Oh, that's so sweet!" Trish said.

"It was. You know how much she loves birds. She gave us three antique life-like robins with wires through their feet so they could be attached to the tree and look like they were perched in it. She told us to be careful with them; they had been passed down to each newlywed couple in the family for years.

"We finished decorating and decided to go pick up some pizza in town for dinner. But while we were gone, Tiger somehow managed to climb our tree, and he 'murdered' one of the robins."

Trish gasped. "Oh no!"

"Oh yes. Mark and I had the family heirlooms for less than twenty-four hours before Tiger took out a third of them."

Megan laughed. "What did Grandma Pat say?"

"We never told her," Mark said, "and she never noticed the

flock of three robins had become only a pair. After that, we kept Tiger and the tree in different rooms."

"You all are sworn to secrecy!" Lois said. "What's shared at Pastor J.D.'s and Trish's stays at Pastor J.D.'s and Trish's!"

"Well, at least your cat didn't knock the tree over when he climbed it," Mary Beth said. "My uncle and his family came to visit us once when I was a kid. We were all chatting in the kitchen when we heard the loudest crash in our living room. We all raced to see what had happened, and my uncle's youngest son had climbed Mom's eight-foot Christmas tree and brought it all the way down to the floor with him. We couldn't find him at first because it had landed on him!"

"Did he get hurt?" Macy asked.

"He was fine, Macy, but I can't say as much for the tree!"

Mattie looked over at Doug and grinned.

He sighed. "I know what you're thinking. Go ahead and tell them."

Mattie leaned forward, her eyes shining. "One year, when our kids were little, we put up the tree, got out the lights, and they didn't work. We had no money for new ones, but Doug assured me he could fix them.

"I believe his exact words were. 'I've totally got this!'

"He worked on them a long time, brought them to me, and told me with all the confidence in the world, 'Try them again!'

"With complete trust in my husband, I plugged them in. A fireball arched all the way out into the living room. I yanked them out of the wall, and he snatched them out of my hands and took them away.

Everyone was so caught up in the story, they didn't notice when Ted did a slow turn and bristled.

"He worked on them and worked on them, and then he finally brought them back, and told me, 'Try them again.'

"I said, 'Nope. Not doing that again. The kids need their mother more than they do a tree.'

"So he plugged them in; I couldn't bring myself to look at first, but when I did the lights worked beautifully, and once we got them on the tree it was gorgeous!"

Everyone started to laugh until Ted shouted, "What's wrong with you people? That's not funny! Do you know how much damage a house fire can cause!"

Mattie was so shocked she didn't know what to say. Doug was about to come to his wife's defense when he saw something else in addition to the anger in Ted's eyes. He saw fear.

*There's got to be a reason for this man's behavior and outbursts that we don't understand.*

He quickly prayed silently for help to say the right thing and then said, "Of course, Ted. You're right. It was extremely dangerous. Mattie and I were just too young to realize how dangerous at the time."

Ted turned to look back out the window, and everyone sat in stunned silence a couple moments more.

Deacon Ken broke the quiet. "I have a pretty good Christmas story, if anyone would like to hear? It's about Christmas cookies."

"Well, we all know I can't resist a good cookie," Pastor Tim said with a chuckle. "I'd love to hear it, Ken."

The tension in the room eased slightly as Ken began his story, but over by the window Ted Carncross glared out into the storm.

## 13

## MEMORIES OF SUGAR COOKIES

"Christmas may be a day of feasting, or of prayer, but always it will be a day of remembrance—a day in which we think of everything we have ever loved." –Augusta E. Randel

"A missionary who came to visit Corners Church years ago told us this story," Ken said, chuckling. "She and her husband lived in Taiwan, and one year she volunteered to bring cookies for their Christmas program at church. She made enough dough for twenty-one dozen cookies and started cutting them out, but when she went to put them into the oven, she discovered it had quit working. They were the only American family in a town of two hundred and fifty thousand people, and she said the Chinese people didn't have ovens. So, she called her American friend who lived about forty-five minutes away, and her friend said to bring the dough over, and they'd cut the cookies out and bake them together. So, she jumped in the car, drove to her friend's house, and they cut cookies and baked them as fast as they could. She didn't get home until eleven-thirty that night.

"She was exhausted, as you can imagine, but she still couldn't go to bed. She needed to decorate each cookie; she wanted to make each one special. Finally, she got all the cookies boxed up and ready to go. It was really late before she got to bed.

"That next day they loaded their car with things they had to take to the Christmas program and drove the forty-five minutes to the church. She didn't realize until she got there that she'd forgotten the cookies, and it was too late to go back and get them!"

"Oh the poor dear!" Edna said.

Tim laughed. "I'm sure she probably felt like crying, but having to eat twenty-one dozen cookies is a problem I wouldn't mind having!"

"Tim." Edna sighed. "You know what your cardiologist said about your diet. You don't want to have another heart attack."

"Sure don't," he said, "but everyone's gotta go sometime, and what a way that would be to go!"

Macy said, "I don't want my dad to have a heart attack either. He had to visit a heart doctor last week."

People looked at each other until Ken asked the question everyone was thinking: "You aren't following in your dad's footsteps with having heart trouble, are you, Davey?"

Davey shook his head. "I'm okay. I had some chest pain, and thought I better get checked out, given my family history. I went to see dad's old cardiologist."

"He's still alive?"

Davey laughed. "Don't look so shocked, Ken. He's getting a little older now, but he says he doesn't want to even think about retiring. And I guess as long as he enjoys the work and can handle the job, why quit?"

"I think a few preachers in this area feel the same way," Pastor Tim said. "I know I did! Your dad too, Davey. Maybe one day even J.D. here will feel the same. He'll probably be eighty before he retires too."

J.D. snorted. "I don't think anyone at Corners Church is going to want to put up with me until I'm eighty!"

"Don't be so sure, Pastor," Deacon Ken said. "Corners Church has a long history of hanging on to its preachers!"

*You might be here until you're eighty,* Trish thought, looking at J.D., *but I might not be.*

The pain behind her right eye hit again, and she put her head on J.D.'s shoulder.

"Is that the end of the story?" Ruby asked. "Did that lady and her husband have to eat all those Christmas cookies?"

Ken shook his head. "No, they didn't eat all of them. She gave most of them away to her friends who lived in the same town she did."

Ken noticed Ruby was furiously working in her notepad. "How are you doing down there, Ruby? You keeping up with all these Christmas stories?"

"I can't write fast enough, Deacon Ken," Ruby said. "So, I'm making a picture book to show the old ladies instead. See?"

She held up her notebook and smiled at all the praise.

"Aren't you getting tired, Ruby?" Beth asked, smoothing her hair out of her eyes.

"Not yet!" Ruby said.

"But it's so late, sweetie. It's way past your—"

Davey squeezed her hand. "I think we can let her stay up just a little longer. It is Christmas after all, and tonight she's making memories she'll never forget."

Ruby looked up at her pleadingly. "Please, Mom? I promise I'm not tired yet."

Beth hesitated and then smiled. "All right you two. Christmas only comes once a year."

Ted had been watching the exchange between Ruby and

her parents with a small smile. But it faded as he turned and looked back out of the window into the darkness, Beth's words echoing in his thoughts.

*"Christmas only comes once a year." Yes, and that's one time too many, because when Christmas comes it brings nothing but pain with it.*

## 14

## BABY JESUS COMES TO TOWN

"The greatest gift we can give others is to tell them about the most wonderful Gift God has bestowed on the whole world." – Billy Graham

"Do you want to hear a story about baby Jesus, Ruby?" George asked.

"Sure!" Ruby said.

"Okay! When I was ten, I lived in a small town in the upper peninsula of Michigan for a short time."

"I didn't know you were a Yooper!" Reece said.

"I sure was, and proud of it, eh?" George said. "I was sad when we had to move. But while we lived there, my family and I attended a little church a lot like Corners Church called Fifth Baptist."

"Fifth!" Reece said. "Your town had five Baptist churches? That seems like a lot for a little town."

George chuckled. "It seemed like a lot to us too; we drove all through town when we moved there, looking for a church, but the only one we could find was Fifth Baptist. So, our first

Sunday there, my dad decided to ask the pastor, Pastor Brown, where the other four Baptist churches were.

"Pastor Brown laughed, and said, 'We're the only church in town.'

"My dad was confused, so he asked the pastor, 'But the sign says this is Fifth Baptist, so why is it called that if it's the only church here?'

"'Pastor Brown said, "Well, the story I was always told was that the church founders thought the town would grow and get more churches; as you can see, that didn't happen, but they had no way of knowing that then. Anyway, they didn't want to look proud, so they didn't want to name this church First Baptist. After some heated debate, they finally settled on Fifth Baptist since they thought it sounded 'humbler and more distinguished.'

"My parents and I loved Fifth Baptist from that first Sunday we went there, and we especially grew to love Pastor Brown and his wife. They were always giving me something, a book, candy. They did the same with all the other church kids; they spoiled all of us. They loved kids but sadly had never been able to have any of their own.

"After we were there for a while, Pastor and Mrs. Brown started acting strangely, though. They began taking more and more Sundays off. They took so much time off between Labor Day and Christmas my parents started worrying Pastor Brown was going to other churches as a candidate to be a pastor somewhere else."

"Why would Pastor Brown want to do that?" Macy asked.

"Pastors leave churches for lots of reasons, Macy, but the reason my parents thought he might be leaving our church was because it was so small, and it couldn't pay him very much."

Macy looked worried. "Our church is really small, and

Pastor J.D., you went away for a long time that one time. Are you leaving?"

J.D. sighed, remembering when a couple years prior he had left Corners Church abruptly to deal with the bitterness, resentment, and anger issues he'd developed during his traumatic childhood, being fired from his first church, and his first wife's death. He wished he'd given those burdens to the Lord and sought the help he'd needed far sooner than he had. He'd not left the church on good terms, but when he'd returned, everyone had welcomed him home. His heart ached that Macy or anyone else from church might have any question he'd want to leave here. This was his home now.

"No, Macy. There's nowhere else I'd rather be."

"Oh good," Macy said, looking relieved. "I'd be so sad if you left."

J.D. teared up, and Trish squeezed his hand.

"Me too, Macy," he said.

"So where were Pastor Brown and his wife going?" Reece asked.

"My parents decided to ask the deacons about it," George said. "But all the deacons would say was they'd gone on personal business.

"Everything came to a head the weekend of the Christmas program. Pastor and Mrs. Brown were gone again on Saturday, the last practice before the program, and no one knew where they were except the one deacon, and he wasn't telling. The only thing he'd tell anyone was they'd be back in time for church on Sunday.

"During that last practice we realized we had a problem. There weren't enough kids to do the manger scene. I was Joseph, and I came up to the shoulder of the high school senior girl playing Mary. There was an eight-year-old who was playing the shepherd, and a sixteen-year-old girl who was playing the angel. But that was it—just the four of us—there were no toddlers or babies to play Jesus. Neither of the girls had dolls we could put in the manger. We asked around, but no one else in the church did either. Since Pastor and Mrs. Brown were gone, we didn't know what to do about a baby Jesus, so finally we decided we were just going to have to leave the manger empty.

"The next day, on Sunday morning, the girl playing Mary and I carefully listened for our cue and walked out of the side room right on time as Pastor Brown read from Luke chapter two verses one through seven. Reece, would you mind reading that for us? I'd be willing to bet the farm Pastor J.D. has a Bible around this place somewhere."

J.D. laughed, picked up a Bible from an end table, and handed it to Reece.

"Sure, I'll read it," Reece said. "Grandma asks me to read it at family Christmas every year. I've about got it memorized.

> "'And it came to pass in those days, that there went out a decree from Caesar Augustus that all the world should be taxed.
> 'And this taxing was first made when Cyrenius was governor of Syria.
> 'And all went to be taxed, every one into his own city.
> 'And Joseph also went up from Galilee, out of the city of Nazareth, into Judaea, unto the city of David, which is called Bethlehem; because he was of the house and lineage of David:
> 'To be taxed with Mary his espoused wife, being great with child.
> 'And so it was, that, while they were there, the days were accomplished that she should be delivered.
> 'And she brought forth her firstborn son, and wrapped

him in swaddling clothes, and laid him in a manger; because there was no room for them in the inn.'"

"Thanks, Reece," George said. "While Pastor Brown was reading those exact verses, 'Mary' and I stood behind the manger. I didn't even see anything was different at first, until I noticed Mary staring down at the manger with the funniest look on her face. I looked down and saw a real live baby in that manger! Cutest, tiniest thing I ever saw! He was sound asleep with his thumb in his mouth. But where had he come from, and what was I supposed to do with him if he woke up?

"Pastor Brown kept reading from Luke: 'And there were in the same country shepherds abiding in the field, keeping watch over their flock by night.'

"Our one shepherd, carrying a toy stuffed sheep, came out of the side room, and spotted the baby. Instead of going and sitting on the platform like he was supposed to, though, he stopped in his tracks, and the angel bumped into him, and her halo fell off. She too stared at the baby and forgot to spread her wings the way she'd done in practice. I heard my mom laugh.

"Pastor Brown smiled and kept reading about the angels bringing good tidings of great joy and the heavenly host praising God. We were all staring at that baby, and the four of us totally forgot we were supposed to sing 'Silent Night' and instead crowded around the baby whispering, 'Whose baby is this?'

'Isn't he cute?'

'How did he get in the manger?'

"'Excuse me, kids,' Pastor Brown said.

"He picked that baby up, cradled it close to his heart, and turned to the congregation. Mrs. Brown came up and stood with him. Her face was glowing.

"He said, 'I know you've all been wondering why we've

been gone so much. We didn't want to say anything until it was final. You know how many years we've been trying to adopt, and how many times it's fallen through. Over the past few months, we've been making trips to the Christian Children's Home. Meet our Christmas gift, our new son!'

"The pews emptied as everyone came up to look at the baby and hug Pastor and Mrs. Brown. He kept holding the baby after everyone sat.

"Best as I can recollect, Pastor Brown said, 'I look at my child, this precious baby, and I know I couldn't give his life to save the best man who ever lived, but God gave his only Son to save not only the best of us but even the worst.'

"I remember tears ran down Pastor Brown's face, and he kissed his baby. Then he said something like, 'I'm amazed at God's awesome love for us. He gave Jesus to die for us, to destroy our sins on the cross. If we repent of our sins and believe Jesus died for us, God gives us eternal life. What a gift that is! We don't deserve it. We can't do anything good enough to earn it. We just accept it, like my wife and I took this precious baby when they put him in our arms. Does anyone here want to accept God's free gift today?'

George cleared his throat; when he spoke again, his voice was husky: "There was one person there who did want that gift, someone who looked at the tears on the pastor's face and the sweet baby in his arms, someone who understood for the first time what God had sacrificed to give him everlasting life. A ten-year-old boy knelt at the altar that day."

"Was it you?" Macy asked. "Were you the little boy?"

George nodded. "I was, Macy. I told God I was a sinner, and I thanked him for Jesus who died in my place so I could live in heaven forever. I left church that day with the best Christmas gift I'd ever gotten before or since, everlasting life."

"I've asked Jesus to take away my sins too, George," Macy said.

"I know you have, Macy, and that makes me happy," George said. "I think everyone in this room loves Jesus, and we'll all live in heaven, together, forever."

*You've forgotten one person in this room,* Ted thought. *I don't love Jesus. And I can't believe he loves me, not after what happened.*

## 15

## THE BABIES, THE MISCHIEVOUS ANGEL, THE TRIKE, THE CHEESE, THE ASHES, AND THE MISSING JESUS

"Christmas may be a day of feasting, or of prayer, but always it will be a day of remembrance—a day in which we think of everything we have ever loved." –Augusta E. Randel

"Anyone else got a story, or are we storied out?" J.D. asked.

As several voices chimed in at once, Trish heard the annoying buzz in her ear that had been troubling her for several weeks and zoned out for a moment. When she could concentrate again, Ken was talking.

"Sounds like we've got a hodgepodge of them, Pastor," Ken said.

"What's hodgepodge mean?" Ruby asked.

"I'm not exactly sure what it means, Ruby," Ken replied. "My folks always used it to mean a mixed-up jumble of things."

"So you gonna draw pictures of the hog pod stories?" Cyrus asked.

Ruby frowned. "I thought Deacon Ken said the word was. . . ." Then she smiled at the old man. "Yep, I am Uncle Cyrus.

When I grow up, and am a writer like Trish, I'll draw my own pictures for my books. I think I'll save a lot of money that way; won't I?"

Trish nodded and shook her head in an unsuccessful attempt to clear her vision. She was seeing two of Ruby.

"Can you draw a baby, Ruby?" Shirl asked.

Ruby nodded.

"Okay, good, because George's story reminded me of when Bud and I found out we were expecting our first baby; we couldn't wait to tell our families and decided to do it at Christmas. We drove two-and-a-half hours to spend Christmas Eve with my family, and after all the other gifts were opened, we handed my mom a card that said her last gift would be arriving late—eight months late. You should have seen her face when she stared at our poorly drawn picture of a baby! I'm sure you would have done a much better job drawing one, Ruby."

Ruby's face lit up as she drew.

"The next day we drove home and did the same thing with Bud's family at his family Christmas. Our baby was the first grandchild on both sides, so it was so fun to share the news with we were going to have a baby with all the out-of-town relatives who were there for both family Christmases."

After all the echoes of "aw!" faded, Valerie said, "You know, I had a Christmas baby."

"Really?" Trish said. "I don't think I knew that."

Valerie nodded. "I woke up very early on Christmas morning, thirty-seven years ago today, and told Chuck I was in labor.

"He called the doctor and said, 'Val thinks she's in labor, but I think she's got gas from the chili I made last night.'

"The doctor told him to get me to the hospital right away, so he did. Our baby was born fifteen minutes later.

"The doctor told Chuck, 'That was quite the gas bubble!'"

Valerie and Chuck looked at each other and smiled.

"Best Christmas present we ever got," Chuck said to her.

"Did you get a baby every time Chuck made chili?" Ruby asked.

Valerie gave everyone a look that said not to laugh. "No, Ruby, and it's a good thing, because Chuck makes chili at least once a month, so I'd have quite a few babies by now!"

"A bowl of chili sure would taste good right about now," Tim said.

Edna gave him the look.

"Just kidding, honey," he said, "but listening to these stories is making me hungry."

"Are you ever not hungry?" she asked.

"You know the answer to that. Hey, Davey, take my mind off being hungry. You got any Christmas stories about your family, maybe that don't involve food?"

"I have more than a few," Davey said. "My sister, April, was two Mom and Dad's first Christmas here. Some of you might remember the wooden communion rail across the front of the church?"

A few people nodded.

"Well, Mom thought it would be cute to dress April like a little angel, tinsel halo and all, and have her come out from the Sunday school room and stand next to Dad while he read the Christmas story. April came out all right, but she didn't stand next to Dad. She yelled, 'Wahoo!' and started swinging off the communion rail. Dad gave Mom the eye, and Mom had to come get her. Everyone in church thought it was hilarious, everyone except Mom and Dad that is!"

Deacon Ken laughed. "I remember that. You know, Davey, my mom used to get so upset every time your mom disciplined April. I remember one time your mom took April outside to give her what for.

"My mom just couldn't take it anymore, so after church, she

finally decided to confront your mom: 'Darlene, what did that poor child do now? I never heard her make a peep!'

"Your mom said, 'She didn't make a peep. She just stuck her tongue out at me.'"

Everyone laughed.

"Since April isn't here, I have another story about her if anyone wants to hear it?" Davey said.

Everyone did.

"You all probably know, Mom and Dad never had much money, especially when we kids were young, but they did their best to make Christmas special. One year, though, Mom and Dad were having an extra hard time coming up with money to buy gifts for us kids. They always liked to give us a 'big' present and a few small things to go with it. They had everything set for my brother and me, but they hadn't been able to afford April's big gift. They were sitting at the kitchen table trying to figure out what they were going to do when there was a knock at the door. Mrs. Kregel, Pastor Kregel's wife, had come over with this huge round of cheddar cheese. My parents knew right then what to do. Christmas morning, April was so happy when she opened her 'big' present and found it was that entire wheel of delicious cheese."

Reece looked perplexed. "Why did they give Aunt April the cheese?"

"Well, you see, there was never a little girl who loved cheese more than your Aunt April, and it was something we couldn't usually afford to get, especially not a kind that was that nice. Until it was gone, Mom would ask April what she wanted for dinner using her cheese, and April was so excited. None of us kids realized until years later how smart Mom and Dad had been. April got a gift she never forgot, and, thanks to Mrs. Kregel, Mom was able to feed our family at the same time."

Deacon Ken chuckled. "Your parents, especially your mom,

were always really good at getting creative when times were tough. And times were often tough for a lot of families back then. I remember one year when Ellen and I were struggling, and we had to scrimp and save hard to get enough money to buy Bobby a special gift. He was finally old enough to ride a Big Wheel. We couldn't wait to see his face when he saw it under the tree. It was a warm winter with no snow, so we kept imagining him riding it outside like the king of the driveway. It didn't exactly happen that way, though. Christmas morning, we all got an unexpected gift—the stomach flu. We managed to drag ourselves out of bed long enough for Bobby to see his trike. Then we all went back to bed, feeling like we'd been run over by a tractor." Ken laughed and shook his head. "Sometimes things just don't work out on Christmas the way we expect."

"You can say that again," Ted muttered, but no one heard him over the sound of wind and ice hitting the windows.

"Oh, Shirl and I know all about that," Bud said. "There was this Christmas party this one time...." He glanced at Shirl.

She sighed. "Oh, go ahead. Some of these people were there and probably remember it anyway."

"Well, they probably don't know you almost killed me afterward!"

"Oh, I did not! Just tell the story!"

Bud cleared his throat. "So, it was a few days before Christmas, many years ago, and Shirl and I were getting ready for a holiday party we were hosting for friends and family. And of course, the house had to look perfect, like no one lived there."

Shirl rolled her eyes.

Bud continued, "You people know guests look for specks of dust on furniture or spots on drinking glasses, right? That's why everyone comes to Christmas parties wearing white gloves, for the dust test."

Shirl poked him. "Bud!"

"What! You run around whenever anyone is coming over acting like the white glove test could happen any time."

Shirl rolled her eyes again. "I certainly do not. Just keep telling the story."

Bud gave her a quick kiss on the cheek. "The house always looks great."

"Well, not that time!"

Bud laughed. "True!"

"What happened?" Macy asked.

"Well, right before everyone was supposed to get there, Shirl spotted a pile of ashes in the fireplace we had both forgotten to clean out.

"She told me, 'Get rid of it, now!'

"I sprang into action. Now mind you, most intelligent folk would have grabbed a Shop-Vac or at least a broom and dustpan. But I was in a hurry; people were going to start coming any second. The Shop-Vac was in the basement, and the broom and dustpan were on the porch, but the ancient Hoover was in the closet."

Edna gasped. "Bud! You didn't."

"I most certainly did. I grabbed the Hoover and started vacuuming up the ash pile. I'd been at it probably thirty seconds when I heard Shirl scream loud enough I bet you could have heard it on Mars. I turned around to see what was wrong. As quickly as the vacuum was sucking ashes out of the fireplace it was shooting them out behind me—that old Hoover's filter had just given up. Wouldn't you know, right then the doorbell rang? The first guests had arrived to a filthy, dusty house. Everyone laughed about it except Shirl who smiled on the outside but kept shooting me looks that could kill."

"Hey," Shirl objected. "I wouldn't say I was that furious!"

"Oh yeah?" Bud asked. "Then why did I have to hide

anything that you could use to murder me with before the guests left?"

As everyone laughed, Shirl sighed, and Bud enveloped her in a huge hug. She squirmed in protest and escaped his embrace, but she smiled and held his hand.

"Well, you may have forgotten to do some cleaning before your guests arrived, Bud and Shirl," Beth said with a smirk, "but at least you two didn't manage to completely lose Jesus."

"What?" Shirl said, looking confused.

"Oh no, Beth," JoAnn said, putting her face into her hands. "Not this story."

"Wait, what happened?" Reece asked.

Beth giggled. "So, when your Aunt Shelly, Uncle Joe, and I were growing up, Grandma JoAnn used to hide the baby Jesus from our manger scene for us kids to find on Christmas morning. Isn't that right, Mom?"

JoAnn nodded, laughing. She knew what was coming.

"Either Mom or Dad would talk to us about how important it was to seek Jesus while Shelly, Joe, and I would be pushing each other to be the first one to find him—"

"Even when you were teenagers," JoAnn said with a twinkle in her eyes.

"Until one Christmas, that fateful Christmas when no one could find baby Jesus. We searched for probably an hour until we got frustrated and told Mom we gave up. She went to go get him when she realized she'd completely forgotten where she'd hidden him. She searched and searched, but he never showed up—even when we were packing away all the Christmas decorations."

"Oh no!" Macy said. "Did you ever find Jesus?"

Beth grinned and said, "Mom, Dad, Shelly, and I were working in the garden in *June* when Joe comes running out of the house yelling, 'It's been six months, but I finally found the baby!'"

The room erupted into laughter.

Beth gasped for air. "You should have seen the look on the face of old Mrs. Wizen who lived next door!"

Ted was trying to ignore the stories; he didn't want to get drawn into the lives of these people or hear any more about a loving God, but he found himself smiling. He barely stopped himself from laughing out loud. He'd been isolating himself from friendship for so many years he'd forgotten how good it could feel to be part of a group, even if he was just standing on the fringe.

## 16

## CHRISTMAS PROGRAMS

"For it is good to be children sometimes, and never better than at Christmas, when its mighty Founder was a child himself." – Charles Dickens

JoAnn tried to stop laughing as she wiped her eyes and said, "Beth, I can't believe you told everyone that!"
    Miles patted her back and said, "JoAnn, should we tell everybody about that Christmas program Joe was in when he was in kindergarten? Do you remember that?"
    She started laughing again. "How could I ever forget?"
    "You tell them," Miles said. "You're the one he embarrassed the most!"
    "Okay, so there I was sitting in the front row because I was the parent who had for some reason decided to volunteer to help with the kids' Christmas play that year. Joe said all his lines perfectly and smiled through all the songs.
    "Finally, the play was over; I was so proud and relieved—all the kids had done a great job. I was motioning for them to come down from the stage, and they all did, except for Joe.

"He stood alone in the middle of the stage and hollered, 'Hey, Mom! That last song was my favorite! Know why?'

"I looked up at him proudly, expecting some wise beyond his years theological answer.

"You could have heard that boy's voice a football field away as he yelled, 'Because it was the shortest one!'

"Of course, the whole church laughed."

The people in the bonus room thought the story was funny too. Most of them knew Joe, Beth's older brother, and it didn't take much imagination to picture him doing that at five years old.

"Maybe Joe should have gone into theatre the way my niece Nikki did," Lois said. "We all knew she was born to be on the stage even when she was only five years old. That year, she was given the opening line for her church's Christmas program.

"It was simple: 'Welcome to our program,' and she had it perfectly memorized.

"But during every practice, she used her time at the mic to improvise additional material.

"People kept telling her, 'Just say the original line, Nikki.'

"On the night of the program, they reminded her again.

"So, Nikki stepped up to the mic and said, 'This is the original,' and then finished her little welcoming speech.

"The problem was when people heard her say 'This is the original,' they all started laughing, and no one heard her line. You know what, though? That laughter made everyone feel at home, even people who came to church only once a year to watch a child or grandchild perform.

"Nikki works in community theatre now with all kinds of people and still has a great way of making everyone feel at home."

"Lois, Edna and I had a few kids like your niece who had their own ideas about what they were going to say or do during

Christmas programs," Tim said. He chuckled. "There was this one time, back when I was pastor at this large church in Lansing—"

"Wait! You were pastor of a church in a city?" J.D. asked. "How did I not know this?"

"It was before I came to Second Baptist or met Edna. And it really was nothing much to speak of—only lasted there six months. I don't think they appreciated my country ways. But I was there long enough for one unforgettable Christmas program!"

Tim's booming laugh filled the room. "The third-grade girls came in dressed with their perfect tinsel halos and white robes, angelically flapping their arms to announce Jesus's birth to the third grade boys who were dressed as shepherds. Instead of being in awe of the angels, the way they'd been taught in practice, one shepherd boy took his cloth off his head and started whipping the others. This started a ruckus with ten little shepherds wrestling and whipping each other with cloths.

"On the other side of the platform, ten little angels continued sweetly singing, 'Angels We Have Heard on High.' I broke up the rumble and ushered the shepherds off the platform, but I was laughing so hard you could hardly hear the angels. The next Sunday, the board politely suggested that maybe me and the church weren't a good fit."

J.D. wiped his eyes and snorted. "It definitely sounds like you weren't a good fit if they wanted to fire you for that, and I'm glad. I can't imagine if you'd stayed there and not been pastor at Second Baptist, or if you hadn't married Edna. I probably would never have met you, and I wouldn't be who I am without you, Tim, and I'm so glad that, now that you're retired, you're coming to church at Corners Church. We love having you here with us!"

Ruby sat on the floor looking down at her drawing of all the kids in the play. "I wish we had lots of kids at Corners Church," she said. "Do you think we ever will, Pastor J.D.?"

J.D. looked down at her sadly, and Trish looked away, consumed for a moment by the nagging worry about their dwindling church attendance.

*Poor Ruby,* she thought. *It can't be easy for her to be the only little kid at church when Tim and Edna's great-nieces and nephews aren't there. What if their parents decide our church isn't the right one for them? She'll be all alone most of the time again.*

Deacon Ken could see J.D. was struggling with how to respond so after a moment he gently said, "Well, Ruby, some years we've had many children at church and other years only one or two. But every child who's ever come here knows they're loved, just like we love you, and when they grow up, they never forget this country church. Just ask your big sister."

Megan nodded. "This place always feels like home."

"When I grow up like Megan, I'll never forget Corners Church either," Ruby said.

*I wish I could,* Ted thought.

"It was the same way at Second Baptist, Ruby," Edna said. "Some years Tim and I couldn't even have a Christmas program because there weren't enough kids. Do you want to know what I'd do then?"

Ruby nodded.

"I'd bring a rocking chair to church and put it on the platform; then I'd gather the few children we had around me and tell them a Christmas story."

"Can you do that for us sometime?" Ruby asked.

"I'd love to, dear."

"I'm sure all the children loved that, Edna," Mattie said.

"I hope so." Edna laughed. "Oh, but I have to tell you about what happened this one year. I was getting ready to tell all the kids a story about a boy and his pet donkey who ended up being the donkey who carried Mary to Bethlehem where baby Jesus was born, and I decided to start the story by asking if any of the children had pets. Huge mistake.

"Only one little boy answered, and he said, 'I had a dog, but it got dead.'

"I froze. I didn't know what to do—where do you go with that one! The little boy started crying, so I prayed for the words, and God helped me. I told the kids how wonderful God's plan was to include giving us pets to love and care for, and if they die, God is there taking care of them. Then I told the children God had a special plan for the donkey in our story."

"Good save, Edna," Trish said. "Very creative too. Maybe you should have been a writer."

Edna noticed Trish was squinting. *I think she still has that headache, but I know she doesn't want me to say anything about what happened in the kitchen.*

"You know, I did want to be a writer at one time," Edna said. "I was always scribbling stories in notebooks. I didn't think anyone had ever noticed, but then one Christmas, when I was in high school, my father gave me the best gift I ever got. He had this beautiful Smith Corona manual typewriter he used for his office work, and he gave it to me. That meant he had to handwrite all his correspondence. I still get tears in my eyes when I remember what a sacrifice that was and how happy Dad was when he gave it to me. His love made me happier than that typewriter."

J.D. said, "My mom used to tell me 'We keep Christmas best when we keep it with sacrifice and love.' And I just remembered something I read the other day."

He grabbed a book from the end table next to him, flipped a few pages, and read, "'Are you willing to believe that love is the strongest thing in the world—stronger than hate, stronger than evil, stronger than death—and that the blessed life which began in Bethlehem nineteen hundred years ago is the image and brightness of the Eternal Love? Then you can keep Christmas.'"

"That's beautiful, J.D.," Edna said.

He closed the book. "Henry Van Dyke wrote it."

"He still livin'?" Cyrus asked. "Maybe we could get 'em to preach for us when you're on vacation. Like what he says. He uses some big words, but he ain't no worse than you."

J.D. chuckled. "Sorry, Uncle Cyrus. He died in 1933 when he was eighty years old, an old man."

Too late J.D. realized his mistake.

"Watch who you be callin' an old man, boy!" Cyrus said.

J.D. tried to backpedal. "I meant he was an old man for *his* time, Cyrus. People back then didn't live as long as people do now."

"You'll never seem old to me, Uncle Cyrus," Marion said, getting up and hugging her uncle. "You look the same now to me as you looked the Christmas I was sixteen, and you and Aunt Chrissy and Grandad and Nana came to dinner after the Christmas program at church. Remember that?"

He scratched his head. "Can't rightly say that I do!"

"Oh, I think you will. Grandad was pretty upset about dinner, and you had to calm him down. Remember now?"

Cyrus nodded. "Oh, that Christmas! Tell the rest of 'em what happened."

Marion said, "Our family had a traditional special Christmas dinner—ribeye roast. We only had it once a year, and that Christmas, we woke up to find the oven element had burned out. We didn't want to give up the roast, so Mom and Dad decided to try roasting it under the broiler because it still worked. About an hour before dinner, Grandad and Nana arrived. Uncle Cyrus and Aunt Chrissy were there too. I can still see Grandad.

"He kept pacing back and forth in front of the oven saying over and over, 'Now daughter of mine, don't you let that roast burn!'

"He kept telling mom to check the temperature of the roast every few minutes and not to let it get above 145 degrees because he liked it medium. Uncle Cyrus finally coaxed him to come into the living room to play a game of dominoes so Mom and Dad could cook in peace!

"It ended up being the best Christmas roast ever. And it turned out to be the last Christmas we had Grandad and Nana with us. I still think of that day every Christmas all these years later and smile and cry."

Trish squeezed J.D.'s hand. *Please, Lord,* she prayed silently, *give J.D. and me more time together so we can make more memories.*

Ted looked out into the darkness and thought, *I've only been remembering the tears, but I know there were smiles too. What I don't know is if it would hurt too much to think about happy times that can never happen again.*

Mattie said, "Marion, I think those are the best kind of memories—the kind that make us smile and cry. I have a story like that from when I was growing up. When I was a little girl, our family budget was thin, which seems to be a theme in the stories tonight." She smiled at Davey and Ken. "Like you said, Ken, it was tough time for a lot of families."

"One year, Mom decided, to save some money, she was going to make homemade gifts for family and friends. So she made doorstops that looked like prairie girls. She filled large glass bottles with sand and covered each with a unique head, dress, and bonnet she made by hand. I fell in love with one, named it Jennifer, and tried many times to carry it to bed with me. Finally on Christmas Eve, Mom did her best to explain to me that this doll wasn't one to cuddle, and we needed to wrap it so she could give it to my aunt the next day. Inconsolable, I went to bed in tears.

"On Christmas morning I woke up and found a sock-doll version of Jennifer tucked next to my pillow. Mom had stayed up all night to make a cuddly replica just for me. Years later, my daughter loved playing with Jennifer so much Mom made her a Jennifer of her own."

"I love that story!" Ruby said. She held up her notebook and showed the room her drawing of a doll.

"That's a beautiful picture, Ruby," Mary Beth said. "Maybe you can draw a picture for me too? I have a story about when I was little. My sisters and I knew one of our gifts would be the same every year, but we always pretended for our mom's sake we didn't know what was in it. Even though our family didn't have much money, Mom decorated a huge box and filled it with every kind of fruit and nut she could find to buy. Then she'd wrap it in beautiful paper and put our names on it. The fruit and nuts lasted for weeks!

"It wasn't until we got older we realized why it meant so much to Mom to give us that big box every year. Her parents had been farmers, and she'd lived through the Depression. The eight kids in her family cherished the only gift they each got each year for Christmas—one apple or an orange. As adults, we talked about that giant box of fruit and nuts. My sisters and both my parents are in heaven now. Sometimes tears run down my face too, Mattie and Marion, when I remember the wonderful times my family shared at Christmas."

"Only one apple or an orange? That's all your mom and her brothers and sisters got for Christmas?" Ruby asked.

Mary Beth nodded. "Not everyone is as blessed as we are, Ruby. Some people don't even have a home to live in. Some of them have to spend the night at shelters, like the warming center where Doug volunteers."

"I'd like to go help at the warming center!" Ruby said.

"I'll remember you said that when you're old enough to help out," Doug said.

"I'm old enough right now. I asked Mom and Dad for a pink and purple blanket and a doll for Christmas," Ruby said. "If I get them, I want you to take them to the center."

Davey and Beth looked at each other with tears in their eyes.

"Hey, you two," Doug said to them, "I see the apple doesn't fall far from the tree."

"I don't know what that means," Ruby said. "But I can draw an apple tree if you want?"

Doug smiled at her. "Thanks, Ruby, but you should save your drawing hand in case there are any more stories."

"I have a story!" Jenna said. "How are you at drawing trucks, Ruby?"

"Not very good, but Reece is. He can help me."

Jenna smiled. "Okay, good, because I have a truck story. South Carolina doesn't usually get much snow, but it did one Christmas. We were going to visit my mom for the holiday and had heard about a big storm coming to the south, so we drove our truck down. It handles snow better than the car, so we packed the six of us in it. We were almost to Mom's before it got really bad. The truck started sliding, and we were coming to a hill, so Dale asked the kids and me if we'd get out of the warm truck and go sit on the icy tailgate to put some weight on the back of the truck. As the truck slowly crept up the hill, we passed a man walking down it. He stopped and stared at us like he'd never seen a woman and four kids riding in the back of a truck in a snowstorm. We were all laughing hysterically, so I'm sure that only confused the poor guy even more. We got to

Mom's safely and made a Christmas memory we laugh about every year."

"Was the truck red?" Ruby asked. "I want to color it red when I get home."

"It actually was," Jenna said. "It looked like a Christmas card truck all covered with snow. The kids and I were covered with snow too and half frozen, but Mom's hot chocolate thawed us out, just like Trish's did when we got here tonight!"

"Ruby," Edna said, "When I was little like you, I liked to color and draw too. Christmas morning, when I was five, Mom handed me a big present. When I opened it, it was only an empty wooden box. I don't remember if I cried, but I sure wasn't happy. Who wants an empty wooden box for Christmas? Then my parents told me to go look in the guest bedroom. When I opened the door, I saw a beautiful little desk waiting for me. One drawer was missing. The drawer was the box I'd opened. I forgot all about being sad when I ran and hugged my new desk!"

"I don't think any of us are going to get presents this year," Macy said. "It's Christmas right now, and we're snowed in here."

"We'll get presents when we all get home, Macy," Megan said. "And being together tonight is a gift. I know better than I used to how special getting to be together is. Sometimes at grad school I get homesick for Corners Church. Like I said earlier, it will always be home to me."

"It feels empty without you and the others your age who grew up here," Trish said. "It would be wonderful if you could all come back for Christmas every year. I love what Marjorie Holmes wrote, 'At Christmas, all roads lead home.'"

Marion sighed. "Megan is right. It is a gift, all being together like this. Won't heaven be wonderful when we'll be able to, as Ruby would say, 'all live happily ever after' and never have to say goodbye?"

Ted folded his arms across his chest, and his eyes filled with tears. *That's all well and good, but what about the goodbyes I never got the chance to say here on earth?*

He wasn't the only one with tears in his eyes. Trish's double vision had passed, but now her eyes were wet.

*I'd like a few more years of happily ever after on earth with J.D. and everyone else I love, Lord, if that's your will for me. But I still mean what I told you during those horrible months when Louise kept me in the root cellar: I choose you. Whatever you want for me is want I want too. But I'm struggling. Help me to mean what I'm saying to you, and help me face the future with faith not fear.*

## 17

## HAPPILY EVER AFTER

"Christmas is a time for miracles, and you are truly a miracle from heaven." –Unknown

George didn't notice Ted and Trish's tears. He was too busy smiling at Marion.

"Speaking of 'happily ever after,' do you remember what you said to me last year at the wedding, J.D.?" he asked.

"How could I ever forget?" J.D. answered, putting an arm around Trish, and pulling her close.

He noticed her tears. "You okay?" he whispered.

"Just hold me," she whispered back. Then she smiled, remembering their special day.

"Well, George, you gonna tell the rest of us what the preacher said to ya?" Cyrus asked.

"Sure, Uncle Cyrus," George said. "When you walked up the aisle last year with two beautiful brides, Trish on your one arm and Marion on the other, I was so happy I could hardly catch my breath.

"Then J.D. whispered something to me I hope I remember as long as I live, 'Here come our happily ever afters.'"

"See!" Ruby said. "I told you all; all the best stories end with 'happily ever after!'"

"That's right, Ruby, they do," George said. He took Marion's hands in his. "And Marion, I've never been as happy as I've been this last year with you."

Ted could see their faces mirrored in the window, two elderly people with white hair still smiling at each other like young lovers. People in love didn't know how lucky they were.

"The story isn't over is it?" Ruby asked. "What about the 'once upon a time' part?"

"What do you mean, honey?" Marion asked.

"You know, the beginning part of the story. What happened? Did George get down on one knee when he asked you to marry him?"

"I did, Ruby," George said, "and I had the worst time getting back up, but it was worth it, because I finally got Marion to say yes. I'd been wanting to propose to her for months, but she didn't want me to until she knew Trish was safe. I understood; we were all worried sick about Trish after she was kidnapped, but it was especially hard for Marion because sisters have a special bond. So, I waited.

"After we rescued Trish from Louise last May, I was holding Marion under the lilac trees in her yard while she sobbed with relief. I almost asked her to marry me then, but I knew it wasn't the right time. So, I prayed instead that God would show me when to propose."

"You prayed about when you should get engaged?" Reece asked.

"I did; I think everyone should. There's a quote that's stuck with me for years that I've done my best to live my life by: 'God gives His very best to those who leave the choice with Him.'"

"So how did you know when it was the right time?" Reece asked.

"Oh, I knew. We finally got the news that Trish was going to be able to come home from rehab on September 15, a beautiful summer-like day. Marion was so excited. She'd spent a week getting the house perfect and cooking all Trish's favorite foods. I told her she needed a bit of a rest and asked her to sit with me on the porch swing while we waited for J.D. to bring Trish home."

"He had a hard time convincing me to stop working," Marion added. "I wanted everything perfect for Trish's homecoming."

"And it was perfect," Trish said. "Our old house had never looked as good to me as it did that day I finally came home."

"Just a few minutes before J.D. got there with Trish," George said, "I took Marion's hand and pulled her out to the swing, sat her down, and got down on one knee. She started crying."

"She cried?" Ruby asked. "Why? Because she didn't want to marry you?"

Marion smiled. "Oh, no, Ruby, I was crying because I was so happy."

"Mom cries happy tears sometimes, but I don't get it," Ruby said. "I only cry when I'm sad."

George smiled at her. "Do you want to know what happened next, Ruby?"

She nodded.

"I took a box with a diamond ring out of my pocket, and then I said—"

Marion took his hand as her eyes filled with tears. "You said, 'No amount of time with you will ever be long enough. But could we start with forever?'"

Trish said, "J.D. and I arrived right after George had put

the ring on her finger. The four of us had a wonderful time that night, planning our double Christmas wedding. It's hard to believe it's been a year already since Marion and I walked down the aisle and saw our 'happily ever afters' waiting for us!"

"Your wedding was beautiful," Megan said. "Trish, I loved the part where Pastor J.D. said to you, 'Christmas is a time for miracles, and you are truly a miracle from heaven.'"

"This is the best story yet!" Ruby said. "And now you all get to live 'happily ever after,' forever!"

Trish's face fell, and she brushed a tear from her cheek. "I hope so, Ruby."

J.D. cupped her chin in his hand. "Trish, what is going on? What is it, babe? Can't you tell me?"

"I will after the holidays," she said. But then she looked at his troubled face and sighed. *I don't think I can put this off any longer. He knows something is wrong, and he's getting too upset.* "Would you all excuse us for a little bit? I think J.D. and I need a few minutes alone in the kitchen to talk."

As J.D. reached down a hand and pulled Trish to her feet, she felt like the room was spinning, and she clung to him for support.

As they left the room, Ted felt something he hadn't in a long time, concern for someone else. *That doesn't look much like "happily ever after" for those two,* he thought.

## 18

# THE PRAYER MEETING

"Dear God, I don't know all of the challenges my friends have, but you know everything. I hear their silence, you hear their prayers. I see their laughter, you see their tears. I see when they give, you see what's been taken from them. I see their beautiful appearance, you see the scars in their soul. I experience their faith, you know their doubts. My prayer for them God is that you hear every single prayer and meet them at their need. In Jesus' name. Amen." –Unknown

No one in the bonus room knew quite what to say or do. People looked at each other worriedly or stared into the fire. The flames were burning low, so Davey got up and put a few more pieces of wood on the fire.

"My dad used to say that alone we're like a twigs, easily broken," he said, "but bundled together we're strong."

A soft murmur of voices came from the kitchen. It sounded like Trish was crying—then they could hear J.D. crying as well.

"That's why our church family is strong," Davey said, a little louder. "We stand together. No one faces trouble alone unless they want to. We don't have to know what Pastor J.D. and Trish are going through right now to stand with them and make them strong. We can pray. Dad also used to say we shouldn't pray God will give us an easy life but that he'll make us strong for the life we have."

Deacon Ken nodded. "Like I've said before Davey, you could be a preacher."

Davey shook his head. "Dad was the preacher. I just remember a lot of what he said."

"When someone at church needed prayer, your dad used to say it was time to circle the wagons," Lois said. "I'm sure you all remember how we'd stand in a circle around the church, hold hands, and pray. We did that that once when my dad was so sick, just before he died."

She brushed away a tear, and Mark put his arm around her.

"Well why don't we do that right now," Pastor Tim said, "and pray for our dear friends."

They formed a circle and held hands. Ted stayed where he was, outside of the circle, listening.

"I'll pray first," Cyrus said. "Lord, it's me, Cyrus Goodright, comin' to talk to you a-gin. I got somethin' to say to you about our preacher and Trish. If I was you, I'd be thinkin' they'd already had more than enough trouble to last two lifetimes, and I wouldn't be lettin' them have no more. But I ain't you, and it's probably a good thing, 'cause I'd be makin' a mighty big mess a things. But, Lord, we love those two people a heap, and if they be facin' more trouble right now, like it seems they be, please get 'em through it. And help the rest of us to stand by and give 'em a hand. That's all I got to say. I'll be talkin' at you more later, but I'm done for now. Goodbye."

Ted saw tears running down Cyrus's face. *I wonder what it would feel like to have anyone who cared that much about me.*

Deacon Ken prayed next. "Lord, we know hard times make us better or bitter...."

*Better or bitter?* Ted thought. *I know what my life has made me. Why did I even go to church tonight? There's no hope for me at this point.* Lost in thought, he didn't hear the rest of Ken's prayer.

Several others prayed, and then Pastor Tim prayed last: "Dear, dear Father, we know you love us. We know every trial faith gets us through makes us stronger to face the next battle, but please...." His voice cracked, and he had to stop to take a deep breath. "I won't ask you to take Trish's and J.D.'s troubles away. I wish whatever is going on, I could take it for them, but I know life doesn't work that way. So, I'll ask you to give them your love, joy, and peace. Keep them from bitterness. Keep them from doubting your love. And Lord, like some old saint once said, if they get tired running the race, show them again the vision of your face...."

J.D. and Trish walked back into the room, tears still fresh on their faces, and saw their friends praying for them. They'd never felt more loved.

After Tim said "amen," Trish smiled at everyone through her tears. "I don't know how to thank you all, but your prayers are already making me feel stronger. I think it's time to tell you what's going on."

## 19

## UNWELCOME NEWS

"O Lord, by all thy dealings with us, whether of joy or pain, of light or darkness, let us be brought to thee. Let us value no treatment of thy grace simply because it makes us happy or because it makes us sad, because it gives us or denies us what we want, but may all that thou sendest us bring us to thee, that knowing thy perfectness, we may be sure in every disappointment that thou art still loving us, and in every enforced idleness that thou art still using us, yea, in every death that thou art still giving us life, as in his death thou didst give life to thy Son, our Saviour, Jesus Christ." –Phillips Brooks

"I'm freezing," Trish said as she and J.D. returned to their place on the floor next to the fire. She lost her balance, and he helped her sit. "Does anyone else want more hot chocolate before we talk about all this?"

J.D. sighed. "Babe, you've been limping more, having headaches, and now the last few days these dizzy spells. I didn't know about your double vision, but I should have known something was wrong. I'm never going to forgive myself—"

"There wasn't anything you could have done." Trish took one of his hands in hers. "I didn't want to scare you." She looked at everyone's faces, and her voice wavered, "I didn't want to scare any of you until I knew for sure it wasn't panic attacks."

"Let's get Trish that hot chocolate," Mattie said to Shirl. "Anyone else want more?"

As Mattie and Shirl hurried to the kitchen, J.D. put his arm around Trish, and she laid her head against his chest.

Macy walked over to Trish with her blanket. "Here. I'm not very cold. You can have my blanket." She covered Trish and then leaned down to hug her. "Will you be warm now?"

"If your hug doesn't make me feel warm, Macy, nothing will."

Trish drank only a few sips of her hot chocolate before she handed her cup to J.D.

"I don't really know what to say," she said, looking sadly at everyone. "I guess I'll start with 'once upon a time,' like Ruby says all stories should start. I'm just hoping and praying my story will end with 'and they all lived happily ever after,' but I don't know. No one does, and I've been to see the smartest people who could tell me.

"I noticed something was going on with me, and I've been seeing some specialists the last few months, locally and at University of Michigan—"

"Trish!" Marion interrupted. "Why didn't you say anything to me? How did you get to these appointments without J.D. or me knowing?"

"Well, you both know I've been trying to get my new book ready to publish, and you know how many meetings that requires with my editor and illustrator. So, when I said I had appointments, you both assumed that's where I was going, and I didn't correct you. I didn't want to worry anyone if it turned out to be nothing. But it is something. The only one who knew before tonight was my editor. I only drove as far as her house, and she drove me to appointments after I started seeing double sometimes, and then there was the vertigo—"

Marion started sobbing. "Trish, I don't understand. We tell each other everything. Why didn't you tell me or at least tell J.D.?"

Trish teared up. "Marion, sometimes I feel like I've been worrying you my whole life, and I didn't want to do it again! I usually tell J.D. everything, but you know he only recently stopped worrying every time I left the house. After everything that happened to me, he always thought there was a kidnapper lurking around every corner, and to be honest, so did I."

"Oh honey," Marion said, sitting beside her and taking her hands. "I didn't know it was so bad."

Trish started crying. "It took me months to get my confidence back and for our marriage to have anything like an ordinary day. I don't know if most people realize what a blessing a boring, ordinary day truly is. I didn't want to give that up until I had to. I hope you can forgive me, Marion. I'm so sorry."

Sounds of sniffling filled the room as the sisters embraced.

After a few moments, Trish pulled away and said, "I didn't know what was happening to me. My hip that Louise had broken was hurting, so much worse than normal. Then I started having headaches and seeing these flashes of light. I tried to ignore it at first, but then I started having these dizzy spells.

"The pain in my hip became unbearable, so I finally went to the doctor. They sent me for so many tests. At one of my appointments, I mentioned my other symptoms, and my doctor sent me to see another set of specialists. Then they did even more tests and scans."

She sighed and looked down. "I only got the final diagnoses and treatment plans earlier this week. I wanted to wait to tell everyone the bad news until after we celebrated Christmas. I didn't want to ruin—"

Cyrus struggled out of his chair. "For the love of Pete, darlin'! Get on with it! I'm 'bout worried sick and not gettin' any younger! I'm like to die of old age before you tell us what is goin' on with ya!"

"I'm sorry, Uncle Cyrus. I have two issues, both caused by what Louise did to me. When she broke my hip, it damaged blood vessels. The bone is dying and collapsing because it isn't get enough blood. It's why I've been limping so much worse lately. It's called avascular necrosis."

"Don't need no big words, Trish," Cyrus said, looking pale. "Just wanna know how they gonna fix it. Don't like the sound of no dead bones."

"I had a consultation this week with two surgeons; they want to do a procedure they've had a lot of success with. People have come from all over the country for it, Uncle Cyrus. They're going to take the smaller bone, the fibula from the bottom of my leg, along with the arteries and veins, and put it up into my hip where the dead part is. It will be a long recovery, but it should fix everything."

"That's fantastic news, Trish!" Edna said. "When will that surgery be happening? Soon?"

Trish shook her head. "No, not right away. I have to have something else done first, something even more serious."

Cyrus started shaking, and he looked ready to collapse. Reece stood and quickly went over to him.

"Why don't you go sit by Trish, Uncle Cyrus?"

Davey stood, got a chair from the kitchen, and set it near Trish. The old man didn't protest as Davey and Reece helped him to the chair. His eyes never left Trish's face. She reached over and squeezed his hand tightly.

"Like I said, they found two things wrong. The pain behind

my eye, the headaches, the flashing light, the vertigo, and the double vision are from an unruptured brain aneurysm."

"What in tarnation is that?" Cyrus asked.

"It's like. . . a bubble, on an artery in my brain, and when blood pushes into it, it can grow and get thinner and eventually pop, or rupture.

"Some aneurysms are small and don't need treatment, but mine is large and thin. It's ready to rupture. It's actually a good thing I had symptoms. Some people don't have any until it's too late. The bad news is my aneurysm is in a tricky spot. I'll need a craniotomy."

"A what?" Cyrus asked.

"They'll have to cut my head open. If they can reach the aneurysm, they're planning to repair it by putting clips on it."

"Like clothes pins?" Ruby asked. "Grandma JoAnn has those."

"Kind of, Ruby, only very tiny ones. If the surgeon can reach the aneurysm, he'll put the clips at the base of the aneurysm so no blood can get into it. Then it will shrink and go away."

"That sounds right dangerous!" Cyrus protested. He began to cry. "Do these doctors know what they're talkin' about? What's goin' to happen to you with them messin' in that beautiful brain of yours? How did this happen to you?"

Trish stood and wrapped her arms around her uncle. "I hate worrying you, Uncle Cyrus."

"I worry because I love ya! That's what ya do when you love somebody, and I been lovin' on you ever since I met you when you was a just a lil' bean sprout. Now you tell Uncle Cyrus how this happened to ya."

Trish sighed. "It happened because of what Louise did. When I tried to get away that one time, she caught me. When she thr—" She paused and looked at Ruby. "When I fell down the stairs in the cellar, I hit my head so hard I passed out. The doctors think it probably happened then."

"That woman," Cyrus said, barely able to talk, "brought such a heap a trouble on this family. Tryin' to forgive her has been the hardest—" He trailed off, unable to speak.

Trish squeezed his hand tighter. "I know, Uncle Cyrus. J.D. and I have really struggled with that as well. We both talk to our therapists about it. I'm not sure I've fully forgiven her myself, but I make an effort, every day, to try. I remember that God loves her, and I ask for his help."

Ted whirled around from his place by the window; his face red. "After what that woman did to you? Why on earth would you try to forgive someone like that. She doesn't deserve it."

His anger surprised Trish; he was a bystander and not personally involved. He didn't even know her.

Trish breathed in deeply. *How do I answer him, Lord?* "Ted, I made up my mind while I was still helpless in the root cellar that I wasn't going to let bitterness imprison me too. I didn't want to let it ruin my life like it had ruined Louise's. I knew she could kill my body, and she almost did, but my soul and spirit were God's; she wasn't going to touch those.

"You don't know me, so you don't know I love to collect and memorize Bible verses and quotes. They've been a light in the darkness to me more than once. Louise kept me chained in that root cellar for weeks. During that time, I kept thinking of something Nelson Mandela had said. I made up my mind if I ever got out alive, I'd do the same thing he did."

She waited for Ted to ask what it was, but he didn't; so, she told him anyway: "Mandela said, 'As I walked out the door toward the gate that would lead to my freedom, I knew if I didn't leave my bitterness and hatred behind I'd still be in prison.'"

Ted said nothing, he just turned away from her.

*I think you've turned your back on God the way you are on me now,* Trish thought. *But you know what happens when you turn your back on the Son of God? The Son shines on your back. I should know; I've been where you are.* Trish prayed silently, *Lord, please help Ted find his way back to you.*

After a moment of silence, Chrissy said, "Trish, are those doctors you're seeing really sure about all this? They really are the best?"

Trish nodded. "Absolutely, Aunt Chrissy. They were very thorough, and I have the best neurosurgeon at U of M."

"Thank God for that," Chrissy said with tears in her eyes.

"Do they think you'll have any side effects, dear, from the surgery?" Edna asked.

"The surgeon said I may have some...."

"Like what?" Cyrus demanded.

Trish hesitated. She'd shared the list of possibilities with J.D. Because of the location of her aneurysm there was a chance it could rupture during surgery. That could cause epilepsy, blindness, stroke, paralysis, even death. There was also a chance the surgeon wouldn't be able to reach her aneurysm; that would mean she'd have to live in limbo, waiting for it to rupture and hoping, living in this rural area, she could get to a hospital before she died. But why tell everyone all that when there was only a chance any of that would happen?

She made up her mind quickly. She wasn't going to share everything right now. She knew they'd be by her side to face it with her, if it came to that.

"I might possibly end up with seizures, Uncle Cyrus," she answered.

The relief washed across the old man's face. "Oh, is that all? Had me a buddy with those. Medications helped him good—sure they will you too, Trish. And it's only a maybe you'll get 'em, right?"

"Yep," she said, hugging him again.

As she did, she and Megan made eye contact. Megan knew exactly what dangers she was facing. Trish silently pleaded for her discretion with her eyes, and Megan nodded.

Trish kissed the top of her uncle's head and looked out at everyone. "After I heal from brain surgery, I'll get the surgery for my hip. It's going to be a long journey."

She sighed. "I'm so sorry. I know I'll be missing a lot of church. And with how few of us are coming now, that will make one less. I hope it won't discourage any of you not having your pastor's wife there."

"I know I'm speaking for all of us, Trish," Ken said. "We're just worried about you. We love you. Take all the time you need to rest and heal."

Trish smiled. "Thank you, Ken. I really think J.D. and I have the best church family anyone could have."

J.D. came and stood next to her. She leaned hard against him and sighed.

"Pain?" he asked.

She shook her head. "Always pain, but what gets to me the most I think is the exhaustion. Being in pain all the time makes me a strange kind of tired. I can't really explain it."

"And you invited all of us over here tonight!" Mattie exclaimed.

"Of course I did. I love you all."

Marion stood and wrapped her arms around her sister again. "Once you sent me a get-well card and wrote an Amy Carmichael quote in it. I loved the quote so much I memorized it, and I want to say it back to you now. 'Life is a battle and always will be; we wouldn't wish it to be otherwise. But I don't like pain for you, or overtiredness. I can only ask Him to fill your cup so full of joy that it will overflow over the tiredness, even as it did for Him when He sat by the well.'"

Trish burst into tears.

Ted stood next to the window, feeling like someone outside looking in. He didn't say anything as he listened to the chorus of well wishes, assurances of prayers, and the expressions of love. People surrounded J.D. and Trish, hugging them and crying.

Then someone started singing, and the rest of them joined in.

> "I'm so glad I'm a part of the Family of God,
>    I've been washed in the fountain, cleansed by His blood!
>    Joint heirs with Jesus as we travel this sod,
>    For I'm part of the family,
>    The Family of God.
>
> You will notice we say 'brother and sister' 'round here,
>    It's because we're a family, and these folks are so near;
>    When one has a heartache, we all share the tears,
>    And rejoice in each victory in this family so dear."[1]

"'When one has a heartache, we all share the tears,'" Deacon Ken said. "That's been true of Corners Church as long as I've been going, and I've been attending a mighty long time. We'll share your tears, Trish and Pastor J.D., and we'll celebrate your victory too."

Trish and J.D. looked at their church family and smiled through their tears.

*This place!* Ted thought. *These people! They act like they live in one of those sappy movies where everything works out just in time for Christmas.* He kept watching them intently, but he didn't feel his usual cynicism; instead an aching loneliness took its place.

Thunder rolled; lightning flashed, and Ken said, "Now we've got thunder snow! This is some storm!"

Suddenly a crash that sounded like an explosion rocked the room and glass splintered everywhere.

## 20

## SHATTERED

"I ask Thee for a thoughtful love, through constant watching wise,
To meet the glad with joyful smiles, and to wipe the weeping eyes;
And a heart at leisure from itself, to soothe and sympathize." –
Anna Waring

Trish rushed as best she could across the room to where Ted lay crumpled on the floor. Megan was already by his side. Her own troubles forgotten, Trish looked down at the unconscious man covered in glass, a tree limb lying on his right leg, and a smaller branch next to his head. His leg was twisted to one side, and Trish hoped it wasn't broken, but the blood pouring from the wound on his head scared her more.

"Do you have a first aid kit?" Megan asked her.

Trish nodded. But J.D. was already there, kit in his hand.

Then he dialed 9-1-1 and explained the situation. "Okay. I understand." He hung up and faced the others. "They'll get here when they can, but right now they're saying it's impossible."

Megan bandaged what turned out to be only a small cut on Ted's head and held pressure on it until the bleeding stopped. But Ted remained unconscious.

"Can someone get these branches off him so I can take a look at his leg?" Megan asked. People worked quickly to move the branches and clean up the glass around the man.

Megan felt the bones in the bottom of Ted's leg. Macy was close by, wringing her hands.

"Megan, is Mr. Ted going to die?"

"No, Macy, I think he's going to be just fine. He'll need x-rays to be sure, but I don't think his leg is broken. He'll probably wake up soon."

While Megan worked, the others began discussing how to cover the broken window. The temperature inside was quickly dropping, even though the fire in the fireplace hadn't gone out.

As they talked, the freezing rain changed to snow, and it began drifting in through the broken window, falling onto the old man's face.

"We need to get that fixed, fast!" Megan called.

Suddenly, Ted opened his eyes and groaned. "What happened? Marsha! Kids! Where are you? Are you alright?"

Megan said. "Try to lie still for a few minutes. A tree fell, and some branches broke the window and hit you. I don't think you're seriously hurt, but it's a miracle you aren't. God was watching over you for sure."

Ted looked up at her, dazed and confused.

"Can he have my blanket, Trish?" Macy asked.

Trish nodded, and Ruby helped Macy cover Ted.

He looked at Macy and Ruby and began to sob. "Girls, hurry and get your mother! We have to get out of this house. Something terrible is going to happen!"

Ruby and Macy teared up.

"What's he talking about, Megan?" Ruby asked. "What terrible thing?"

"He's scaring me!" Macy said.

"Come here, girls," Beth said, pulling her daughters away. "It's okay. Ted hit his head. He's confused. Come over by me, and let Megan work."

Ted stared up at Megan and slowly became more lucid.

"I. . . I got confused. I thought your sisters were my girls. Did I scare them?"

"They'll be fine, Ted," Megan said. "It's okay. I need you to lie still for me."

"Marsha and the girls, gone, gone forever, and on Christmas Eve too. A night just like tonight. Horrible storm."

He groaned, then sobbed.

## 21

## THE STRANGER REVEALED

"Kindness. The most valuable gift you will ever give someone."
–Unknown

Ken, Mary Beth, Cyrus, and Chrissy exchanged glances and hurried to the kitchen.

"Ted Carncross my foot!" Cyrus whispered loudly.

"Hush!" Chrissy scolded. "You don't want him to hear you."

Tim and Edna joined the group in the kitchen.

"You've figured out who he is too, haven't you?" Edna asked.

Ken nodded. "It was so long ago; no wonder we didn't recognize him. What's it been, thirty years? That's Ronald Taber in there."

Mary Beth's eyes filled with tears. "That poor man."

Megan came into the kitchen, and Chrissy asked, "How's Ronald?"

"Who?"

"That man's real name is Ronald Taber, Megan," Ken said.

"Wait, then why did he tell us his name was Ted?" Megan asked.

"I'm not sure," Ken said. "Trauma, maybe? My guess is he just didn't want us to know who he was because then we might ask questions."

"Questions about what?" Megan asked.

"About thirty years ago, Ronald's home, not far from here, blew up in a terrible gas explosion on Christmas Eve. Ronald was outside shoveling snow. His wife, Marsha, and his two daughters, about the ages of Macy and Ruby were inside. So was a cat the whole family loved. People miles away heard the explosion and saw the flames. A neighbor found Ronald just outside the door, unconscious, with third degree burns, and pulled him to safety, but his family and the cat were gone. There was no saving them."

Megan gasped. "I've heard about that! Grandpa Miles told me. That explains why he kept talking about Marsha, and he thought Macy and Ruby were his girls. I wouldn't be surprised if he has a concussion. Wait, didn't his whole family attend Corners Church? Why didn't anyone recognize him?"

Ken said, "It's been thirty years since anyone has seen him, though, Megan, and those scars. . . . We just didn't realize it was him. After the fire, Ronald was in the burn unit at University of Michigan Hospital for a long time. Pastor Jim and Darlene visited him often, and many of the rest of us did too. But he wouldn't talk to any of us, and he finally told the nurses not to let any of us in his room. We never heard from him again. One rumor said after he got out of the hospital he moved to Detroit."

"Why do you think he's here now?" Megan asked. "I wonder what made him come back after all these years, and why wouldn't he tell anyone who he was? Was the fire his fault?"

Cyrus shook his head no. "T'wasn't no one to blame for that. One of them 'freakish accidents' as they say. LP tank too close to the house sprung a leak. It blew and took the whole house with it. A tragedy, but no one could have stopped it or helped old Ron's family neither."

"I should get back in there," Megan said. "I've got to monitor him to make sure he's doing okay until the paramedics can get here. Who knows how long that will take with the roads like this."

The others followed Megan back to the bonus room and saw the broken window was covered with thick cardboard and strapping tape. Fortunately, the wind had begun to die down.

J.D. turned on the outside lights, and several people gasped. The white covered landscape looked like a beautiful Christmas card.

Trish was sitting in a chair watching Ted who was sleeping.

Megan put her hand on Trish's arm and said, "Hey, I've got this. I'll watch him. You need to make sure you don't overdo."

Trish tried to protest, but Megan squeezed her hand. "Please, Trish?"

Trish sighed and reached for J.D. who hurried to help her stand. She leaned against him and looked out into the illuminated yard.

"It really does look like a silent night now, doesn't it?" she asked.

"It does," he said. "And I think it's about time we try to get a few hours of a silent night's sleep before the sun comes up."

Yawning, people headed for sleeping bags, recliners, cots, couches, and warm blankets. Tim and Edna took J.D. up on his offer and headed for the bedroom.

"Hey, you two," Trish called after them, "feel free to borrow our pajamas if you can find any that fit."

"Might just do that," Tim said.

"What about you, Megan?" J.D. asked. "Do you need help with Ted so you can get some sleep?"

Megan shook her head. "Like I told Trish, I've got this. I'll stay up with Ted—I mean Ronald. I'm used to pulling all-nighters studying for exams."

"Who's Ronald?" J.D. asked.

Ken and Mary Beth pulled J.D. and Trish aside and quietly filled them in.

Ruby sat up in her sleeping bag and yawned. "Why did you call Mr. Ted Ronald, Megan? His name is Mr. Ted."

"Go to sleep, Ruby," Megan whispered. "We'll talk about it in the morning."

A deep, comforting silence fell over the bonus room.

∼

MEGAN WOKE Ronald periodically to check on him. His pupils were the same size, so she wasn't too concerned, but she wanted to be sure he was okay.

Just before sunrise, a full moon rose. Ronald woke and glanced around. His eyes were clear. He looked at Megan.

"I thought I heard them singing, Marsha and my girls. But it was only a dream. They aren't really here, are they?"

Tears in her eyes, she shook her head.

"But they're somewhere better?"

"They are."

"With Jesus," he whispered and then fell back asleep.

Megan looked at him closely. *Is... is he really?*

Ronald was smiling in his sleep.

## 22

## CHRISTMAS MORNING

"Although it's been said, many times, many ways, Merry Christmas to you!"—The Christmas Song

Trish, a morning person, was the first one awake in the bonus room except for Megan who was still watching her patient and hadn't slept at all. The sun was pouring in the east windows. Trish smiled at Megan, whispered her usual morning prayer of thanksgiving, and looked for Cass. He was curled up next to Ronald, and the old man had his hand resting on the cat's back.

*What is that incredible smell? Coffee? And... pancakes!*

Someone had to be cooking. Trish looked around the bonus room; everyone but she and Megan were still sleeping; it could only be two other people.

*Tim and Edna. Of course.*

Trish slipped out of her sleeping bag grateful not to feel dizzy. She tiptoed over the sleeping bodies into the kitchen where Edna had a massive pile of pancakes ready to put into the oven on the warm setting. A pot on the stove was bubbling and smelled wonderfully like a spicy syrup, but Trish was confused. She knew she didn't have a drop of syrup in the house.

Edna's cheeks were pink, and she looked adorable wearing Trish's snowman pajamas and a red apron well dusted with flour.

"You don't mind me cooking, do you?" she asked.

"Mind? I think it's wonderful! But where did you get that syrup?"

Tim turned from the coffee maker, and Trish stifled a laugh. He'd borrowed a red and white striped pair of J.D.'s pajamas. They barely buttoned, and the sleeves and legs had been rolled up many times.

"You know Edna, Trish. She's a miracle woman in the kitchen."

"I guess so!" Trish went and hovered over the bubbling syrup. "Do I smell cloves?"

"Close," Edna said. "When I couldn't find any syrup, I saw you had a gallon of cider in the fridge. I hope you didn't have plans for it. I mixed brown sugar, cornstarch, allspice, nutmeg, and added the cider. Do you think it's enough syrup for all of us?"

Trish thought it was enough pancake syrup for half of Hillsdale County, and she didn't say she'd been saving the cider to make hot cider for J.D. for Christmas.

"I'm sure it will be plenty, and it smells delicious. Did you make up that recipe just now?"

Edna shook her head, and her white curls bounced. "I saw it in a magazine and have been wanting to try it. I couldn't remember the exact ingredients, so I had to guess." She offered Trish a bit on a spoon. "Here, try some. Blow on it first, it's hot! What do you think?"

"It tastes like Christmas! I can't wait for everyone to wake up so they can try this! Let me help you with the pancakes. After they're done, I'll wake J.D. and get him to whistle to wake up the rest of them."

Tim said, "Better not do that. No whistling! Might give someone a heart attack!"

Tim laughed his famously loud laugh and after that they didn't have to wake anyone up.

Soon everyone but Ronald, who was still sleeping, was sitting where they'd sat the night before when the snowed in adventure had begun. Ken shared Ronald's tragic story, and there were more than a few tears.

J.D. prayed for Ronald and the food, and then everyone dug into the Christmas feast Edna had made, only this time instead of balancing steaming bowls of pasta they were holding plates of pancakes dripping with spicy apple syrup and sipping steaming cups of coffee. Most had added Edna and Trish's favorite creamer, Italian Sweet Cream, but there were a few holdouts for black coffee. Ronald, who had finally woken up and joined them, was one.

He was quiet as the others laughed and talked, but he smiled often, and, despite his ordeal, looked ten years younger than the man who'd walked in the door the night before. Cass curled around his feet.

"Ronald," Trish said, "It looks like you've made a friend for life."

He looked at Cass and said, "I guess I have. And since you just used my real name, I'm assuming you know my story. I was going to tell you this morning, but I have to say I'm more than a little relieved I don't have to. It isn't easy to talk about. That's why I didn't use my real name at church. I apologize for lying to you about my name and about why I was there. I wasn't lost in the storm. I came on purpose. I thought maybe I could find some peace, or some closure, or something. Honestly, I was ready to give up on life. Coming here was my last hope, and I didn't think I'd found it, but I guess I have."

J.D. said, "None of us can even begin to imagine how hard this time of the year must be for you."

This time Ronald was the one who found himself surrounded with an outpouring of love and concern.

Cyrus said, "Whatcha think if'n I was to pray for ya?"

Ronald thought for a moment, and then replied, "I think I'd like that."

By the time Cyrus finished his prayer, tears were running down Ronald's face.

Ruby and Macy approached him, and Ruby said, "Mr. Ted, I mean Mr. Ronald, Macy and I are so sorry about your family."

He held out his arms and both girls gave him a hug.

"Do you still hate Jesus?" Macy asked. The girls had brought their food closer to him and were sitting on the floor at his feet.

"Macy." He chuckled. "Did I ever say I hated Jesus?"

"Not exactly," she said. "But I could tell."

"I suppose everyone could tell." He sighed. "I hated him for a long time, thirty years. My family and I had trusted Jesus as Savior and had lived our lives loving him and others. I couldn't understand why he'd let something so horrible happen to us."

"Why would God let that happen?" Reece asked.

J.D. said, "It's a hard thing to wrap your mind around—hard for me too. Sometimes bad things happen to the best people." He glanced over at his wife, and a lump formed in his throat. "God never promised to keep Christians safe from every bad thing that happens. He just promised to stay with us, help us through it, and he can even bring good from terrible circumstances. He often does protect us, but not always in a way that seems obvious. Everyone goes through trouble of some kind. Do you understand that?"

Reece nodded. "I think so."

Ronald said, "I understood what Pastor J.D. is saying at one point, but after my family died, I was so angry. I didn't want God to help me through it. I needed someone to blame, so I blamed him. I tried to shut God out of my heart and my thoughts, but he kept coming back. I'd remember a song, a Bible verse, something Pastor Jim had said. I knew it was the Holy Spirit reminding me. I guess maybe it was God prompting me to come back to the Christmas Eve service last night.

"You know, I recognized some of you right away too," he said smiling over at where some of the older members of the congregation were sitting together, "but I didn't want any of you to know who I was. I was worried you'd try to talk to me about Marsha and the girls or ask why I'd stayed away for so long."

"Cyrus said, "You came back cause God was callin' you to come on home."

"Maybe you're right," Ronald said. "But when I walked through those doors last night, all I wanted to do was argue with God. I sure wasn't ready to listen."

"Well, you comin' home to God or not?" Cyrus asked.

J.D. winced. This wasn't the approach he'd use, but to his surprise Ronald laughed.

"I came home to God last night when you all thought I was asleep. I woke up this morning without bitterness for the first time in thirty years, and it was a good feeling.

"The stories you told, the love I saw here...."

He glanced at Macy and Ruby and choked up. "And you girls... you'll never know how much your kindness meant to me."

Case rubbed up against the man's ankles, and Ronald laughed.

"And even this cat!"

Cyrus patted him on the back. "So Cass helped ya, huh? He's real good at that. Now that you've come home to God, what ya think 'bout comin' home to the rest of us?"

"I thought about that too," Ronald said. "I wondered if it would be too hard to move back to this place where I have so many terrible memories, but listening to you tell your stories I realized two things. I have many good memories too. And I miss having a family. I think I'd like to be part of the family at Corners Church again, if you'll have me."

"I could call you Uncle Ronald!" Ruby said.

He smiled. "I like the sound of that."

"Speaking of sound," J.D. said, "listen, everyone. Is that what I think it is?"

Reece ran to windows to look. "There's a snowplow coming down Tamarack Road!"

"But I don't want to go home," Macy said.

Beth looked at her, astonished. "But Macy, what about your presents! And you're my little homebody; you love home!"

"I do love home, but this is so nice," Macy said.

"It is, isn't it?" Trish said. "I'll go see if we have anymore coffee because until a plow comes down Lickley Road, we're still snowbound."

"One is coming now!" Reece said. "You guys should see how much snow that plow is throwing."

Everyone hurried to the windows.

Megan looked down the road and frowned. "Still no ambulance."

"What ambulance?" Ronald demanded.

Megan looked at him and raised her eyebrows.

"Wait, for me?" Ronald protested. "No! I don't need one!"

"You need to get checked out at the ER," Megan said. "I'm pretty sure you may have a concussion, and you need to get an x-ray on that leg, just to make sure everything is okay. If an ambulance doesn't show up soon, one of us could take you to the hospital? We all have four-wheel drive vehicles."

"Even with four-wheel drive, we still can't get out," Mary Beth commented. "Did you guys see that parking lot? It's impossible."

Davey pulled out his phone. "Don't worry about that," he said. "I know a guy."

Reece laughed. "Dad always knows a guy."

It was almost lunch time before Davey's guy finished plowing the parking lot and everyone got their cars shoveled out. They gathered back inside Trish and J.D.'s for goodbyes.

"I almost hate to leave," Reece said.

"Will you pray for us before we go?" Ronald asked J.D. "And will you say that benediction the way you did at church last night? Did you know that's the same one Pastor Jim used to say? I never felt closer to God than I did years ago sitting in a pew at Corners Church, seeing Pastor Jim raise one hand just like you do, and saying those words."

"Of course," J.D. said.

The church family formed a circle, and J.D. prayed a prayer so full of love the angels hovering over the little home smiled. Then, raising his right hand, he quoted, "Now unto him that is able to keep you from falling, and...."

Partway through the benediction, Trish opened her eyes. Ronald was whispering the words with J.D., just as he had the night before, and Cass was winding himself around his feet and purring.

J.D finished: "To present you faultless before the presence of his glory with exceeding joy, to the only wise God our Savior, be glory and majesty, dominion and power, now and ever, amen."

"Finally!" Megan exclaimed.

"What?" J.D. looked confused.

"Oh!" Megan laughed and her face reddened. "I didn't mean your prayer. I meant finally the ambulance is here!"

The paramedics came into the house, and Megan briefed them.

Everyone followed Ronald to the ambulance.

"You've all been so kind," he said. "I hate to ask for one more thing, but can someone drive my car to the hospital so I can head back to Detroit after they check me out?"

Trish looked over at J.D. They might have been married only a year, but he knew what that look meant.

"Trish and I have another idea," he said. "After the hospital releases you, would you like to come back here and spend the rest of Christmas Day with us? The roads will be better for travelling tomorrow."

Ronald's face glowed. "Really? You're sure?"

"We're sure," J.D. said. "No one should spend Christmas alone. And we'd like to get to know you better. Have the hospital call us when they're finished with you, and we'll pick you up."

"How will they know your number?" Ronald said, looking perplexed.

"Small town, remember?" Trish said, smiling.

Ronald laughed as the paramedics loaded him into the back of the ambulance, and the congregation waved as the ambulance took off down the snowy road.

"You know what J.D.?" Tim bellowed. "We'd all like to get to know him better. How about if we meet back here at your place at say, seven o'clock, and make it a potluck? The hospital ought to be done with Ronald by then. If not, we could have a potluck tomorrow!"

Edna poked him. "Tim, it's Christmas! We've already spent so much time here; that's rude!"

"I'm glad he was rude because I wanted to come back too," Ruby said. "Now I don't have to be rude and ask."

"Ruby!" Beth groaned.

Trish laughed. "A potluck sounds wonderful!"

"But only if you don't do any cooking, Trish," Tim said. "Let us the rest of us bring the food. Besides, I don't think you have any food left in the house!"

Trish laughed. "Okay, sounds good to me. See you all around seven!"

J.D. and Trish walked back into the house. He pulled her into his arms. "Tell me honestly, babe, how scared are you about everything—the diagnoses and the surgeries?"

"I'm not as worried as I was before. Love was strong here last night, wasn't it? It helped me and brought a prodigal son home." She laughed and nodded at Cass, curled up, sound asleep on the couch, looking satisfied with himself. "And that cat helped bring him home too! You don't think Cass knew what he was doing, do you?"

J.D. shrugged. "Who knows? I think Cass knew Ronald was a man who desperately needed love."

"Everyone needs love," Trish said softly. "And love and prayers will help me through whatever I have to face."

"You can always count on me for those two things, babe. Let's go stand under the mistletoe."

She laughed. "We don't have any mistletoe this year, remember? The store was out."

"We don't? Well, that means any place at all is good for a Christmas kiss."

When he stopped kissing her, she asked, "J.D., do you think we can stay at Corners Church until we're eighty years old?"

"Would you like that?" he asked.

She nodded. "I can't imagine being anywhere else at any

time, especially at Christmas. I don't think any other church has anything like a Corners Church Christmas."

J.D. looked at the piles of blankets and sleeping bags still scattered on the floor and laughed.

"You're right, babe. I think we can safely say no church anywhere had anything like our Corners Church Christmas. Should we make it a tradition?"

Trish didn't even hesitate. "Sure. Why not?"

"You're wonderful; you know that?"

He expected another kiss but didn't get it. Instead, she started to pull away from him.

"Hey! Where are you going?"

"I just had an idea for my book! Make some more coffee, will you?"

"But... it's Christmas! Don't you want to open our gifts?"

"In a minute. I better write this idea down before I forget. Do you mind?"

She smiled up at him, red curls tumbling down over blue eyes, freckles standing out on her beautiful face. He felt his heart flip.

"Nope, I don't mind, babe. Take all the time you need. But I think there's only enough Italian Sweet Cream left for one cup. I just might use it up."

She just laughed. They both knew he wouldn't. He loved her too much.

∼

The End

# NOTES

## 19. Unwelcome News

1. https://www.hymnlyrics.org/newlyrics_f/family_of_god.php

# ABOUT THE AUTHOR

When Donna was a child, she said she wanted to be a writer and a hermit.

Donna achieved both childhood goals. She sold her first short story in 1973. Since then, she has sold more than 3,000 articles and short stories and has published eight books. This will be her ninth.

Donna outgrew the desire to be a hermit but had to be one for three years while she was fighting a stubborn cancer.

*A Corners Church Christmas* is the fourth book in the Life at the Corners series. It's a standalone novel but follows *Corners Church, If the Creek Don't Rise,* and *The Lights of Home.*

Donna has written another series of books, *Backroad Ramblings.* There are currently three volumes available with more to come.

Donna has also published two children's picture books, *The Tale of Two Snowpeople* and *The Tale of Two Trees.*

Donna lives in Michigan with her pastor husband where they have served in the same country church for forty-nine years. Donna enjoys spending time with family, reading, and, when her health permits, camping and hiking.

Donna is a member of American Christian Fiction Writers.

If you enjoy any of Donna's books, please consider leaving a review on Amazon.

Follow Donna's blog at backroadramblings.com.

Find out more about Donna on Facebook at "Donna Poole, author."

Printed in Great Britain
by Amazon